TAMARA WAS BESIDE HERSELF
WITH EXCITEMENT

"Naomi just called me. She and Stephen went to the park together this afternoon. Margaret! They held hands and then . . . THEY KISSED!"

Margaret's heart was beating quickly. She envisioned Stephen's arms around Naomi, clasping her to him, their eyes tightly shut, their kiss long. Just like on television. It was too horrible to think about. But Margaret couldn't stop dwelling on the image she had conjured up. What did Naomi do afterwards? Probably went home and brushed her teeth. Why was Tamara so excited anyway? Big deal!

But Margaret's heart was pounding and her stomach was jumping and she knew she was excited, too. . . .

YOU'RE GOING OUT THERE A KID,
BUT YOU'RE COMING BACK A STAR

"Easy, enjoyable reading."

—*ALA Booklist*

"A wry and honest approach to pre-adolescent growing pains. . . . Young readers will find a lot that they can identify with here."

—*Children's Book Review Service*

THE AGAINST TAFFY SINCLAIR CLUB
by Betsy Haynes
ANASTASIA KRUPNIK by Lois Lowry
ANNE OF GREEN GABLES
by L. M. Montgomery
BANANA BLITZ by Florence Parry Heide
BANANA TWIST by Florence Parry Heide
BE A PERFECT PERSON IN JUST THREE
DAYS! by Stephen Manes
THE DOWNTOWN FAIRY GODMOTHER
by Charlotte Pomerantz
ME AND THE WEIRDOS by Jane Sutton
MIRANDA IN THE MIDDLE
by Elizabeth Winthrop
TAFFY SINCLAIR STRIKES AGAIN
by Betsy Haynes

You're Going Out There a Kid, But You're Coming Back a Star

★★★

by Linda Hirsch

Illustrated by John Wallner

A BANTAM SKYLARK BOOK®
TORONTO • NEW YORK • LONDON • SYDNEY • AUCKLAND

This low-priced Bantam Book
has been completely reset in a typeface
designed for easy reading, and was printed
from new plates. It contains the complete
text of the original hard-cover edition.
NOT ONE WORD HAS BEEN OMITTED.

RL 4, 008–012

YOU'RE GOING OUT THERE A KID,
BUT YOU'RE COMING BACK A STAR

A Bantam Book / published by arrangement with
Hastings House, Publishers

PRINTING HISTORY

Hastings House edition published May 1982
Bantam Skylark edition / October 1984

Skylark Books is a registered trademark of Bantam Books, Inc.
Registered in U.S. Patent and Trademark Office and elsewhere.

ISBN 0-553-15272-6

Published simultaneously in the United States and Canada

Bantam Books are published by Bantam Books, Inc. Its trademark, consisting of the words "Bantam Books" and the por-
trayal of a rooster, is Registered in U.S. Patent and Trademark
Office and in other countries. Marca Registrada. Bantam
Books, Inc., 666 Fifth Avenue, New York, New York 10103.

PRINTED IN THE UNITED STATES OF AMERICA

O   0 9 8 7 6 5 4 3 2

For Warren

☆ 1 ☆

"Pencils down. Books closed!"

Margaret Dapple reluctantly dropped her pencil and turned over her test booklet. Science was getting harder all the time. Who could remember all those people who went to the moon? Neil Armstrong was the first man. Margaret was sure of that.

"Who'd you say was the first one on the moon?" Margaret's best friend Tamara asked her as their teacher, Mrs. Kopelman, was arranging all the test papers into a neat pile.

"I put Neil Armstrong."

"Oh, brother. I knew it was something like that!" Tamara wiped her hands on her beautiful pink and gray flared skirt. "I put Neil Diamond."

Margaret and Tamara began to giggle. Jeffrey Lippman, the class president, was in front of the room letting the best behaved kids get their coats. Margaret and Tamara were usually picked toward the middle. But today Margaret was in a hurry to get home. She sat up straight and folded her hands.

Slowly the class lined up according to size. Margaret was second in line and Tamara was two people behind her. At exactly ten to three Mrs. Kopelman led them down the stairwell. Margaret was bursting with impatience. Mrs. Kopelman seemed to take forever to walk down the steps. If she took this long during a fire drill they'd all be dead! After what seemed like enough time to draw a map of South America and all its products, Class 5-1 finally spilled into the courtyard.

"Are you coming to Susie's to work on the George Washington play?" Tamara called to Margaret.

The Washington play? Who cared about that? That was kid stuff.

"I can't," Margaret called over her shoulder as she headed for the street. "I have to go right home."

Margaret rushed along 187th Street. She didn't even stop at Fred's Stationery Store to buy a candy bar or a comic book. Not today. This afternoon her big sister Barbara was taking her to the movies, and Margaret could hardly wait. Her feet moved even faster. Margaret loved going places with her sister. So what if Barbara pretended she wasn't there. Margaret didn't care. Just walking into the theater with those teenage girls instead of her Mommy and Daddy was worth it all.

Margaret turned down Ft. Washington Avenue. She jumped the three steps in the courtyard that led to her building's brass front door, pushed it open and raced through the lobby to the rear elevator. Its door was already open, as if it had been waiting for her. She pushed 5, impatiently tapped her feet until the elevator reached the fifth floor, and ran out and rang her bell. Barbara let her in.

"I'm on the phone." Barbara held the door open just long enough for Margaret to walk in. Then she hurried back to her room.

Margaret dropped her books on the foyer table and flung her jacket over a chair. How long was Barbara going to stay on the phone? They might be late for the movies. The low murmur of Barbara's voice drifted into the foyer. Maybe she was about to hang up. Or maybe she wasn't. Margaret strained to hear her sister's words, but Barbara was practically whispering. Why was she speaking so softly? What was she up to?

Margaret tiptoed quietly toward Barbara's room and flattened herself against the wall outside. If Barbara saw her she would kill her. Margaret had been caught eavesdropping before—by everyone in her family. She had even been caught eavesdropping by her grandmother, who only came to visit. But Margaret had good reasons for eavesdropping. She figured that when people were whispering on the phone, they were telling secrets. And if they had secrets she should know about them because they might affect her. And this time she was right. Margaret Dapple was listening to her own sister plotting against her.

"I won't do it. No one can make me!" Barbara hissed.

Make her what?

"After all, I'm fourteen—why should I drag a ten-year-old everywhere I go? Meet me at four o'clock. We'll go to the movies alone."

Go to the movies alone? What was Barbara saying?

"My parents will take her some other time. They never let her suffer."

Margaret was getting angrier by the minute. She walked into the kitchen and waited for Barbara. She'd be in pretty soon to feed that big stomach of hers. Margaret hid the last two Mallomars in the tea canister. Sure enough, in a few minutes, Barbara walked in and headed right for the Mallomars.

"Anything good to eat around here?" Barbara picked up the empty Mallomar box. She turned it upside down and shook it. Finally convinced that it was truly empty, she threw it on the table and began opening the cabinets looking for something else.

"What's new, Barbara?" Margaret's hand was wrapped tightly around her milk glass. Her fingers were turning red.

"Not much." Barbara opened the freezer.

How could she act so casual? Margaret was fuming.

"You big liar!" Margaret blurted out. "You're not taking me to the movies. That's what's new!"

Barbara whirled around. "You listened in on my conversation! I'm telling Mommy!"

"Just wait till I tell her you were planning on going to the movies without me. After you promised! See how she likes that!"

"You're not going with me to the movies no matter who you tell! Get it?"

"Oh yes I am!" Tears were running down Margaret's face. "You promised!"

"I did not promise. I said *maybe!*"

"You said *definitely!* I remember! You promised!"

Margaret grabbed the Mallomar box and threw it at Barbara. She missed and hit the bottom of the refrigerator.

"Take off your blindfold!" Barbara taunted.

Margaret was frantic. All she could sputter was, "You promised! You promised!"

At that moment, Mrs. Dapple came rushing into the kitchen. She dropped her coat on a chair and looked at her daughters.

"That's enough! The whole neighborhood can hear you! Why is it always my children arguing?"

The two sisters stopped fighting for a moment to confront their mutual enemy. Mrs. Dapple was standing between them looking much like a referee about to send each contender back to his corner.

"Can't you be friends? You're sisters. You're related!"

"Don't remind me," Barbara mumbled under her breath.

Margaret glared at her and turned to their mother.

"Ma, Barbara swore she'd take me to the movies today. She's going with her friends, and she won't take me!"

"It's not fair! Why do I have to take her every place I go? Not one of my friends has to bring a baby sister along!"

"I am not a baby!"

"Ma, she embarrasses me! Please don't make me take her." Barbara gave her mother a pleading look.

"What can be so embarrassing about taking your sister to the movies? I'm sure your friends don't mind her being there."

"Oh, yes they do! Last time she came along I had to take her to the bathroom three times— once during a love scene! She stepped on everyone's feet and knocked over Lisa's soda."

"I don't like to go to the movie bathroom alone," Margaret defended herself. "There are mean older girls in there smoking, and they look at me funny."

"Who can blame them?" Barbara retorted. She gave her mother another pleading look. "Mom, don't you know psychologists say it's damaging for the older sibling to be responsible for the younger one?"

This was too much! Margaret was furious. Ever since Barbara had decided she was going to be a psychologist, she used psychology to win all arguments. "Don't let her get away with that, Mom!"

"I don't expect you to take Margaret every place you go, Barbara. But you did promise to take her today. And a promise is a promise."

"Go ahead! Take her side! Everyone always does. Just because she's the baby! Well, I hope she gets scared to death today." Barbara wheeled around to confront her sister. "Because we're going to see one of the scariest horror movies ever made! It's all blood and guts!"

"You picked that one on purpose because I don't like scary movies!" Margaret was purple with rage.

"I did not. It's not my fault you're such a baby."

"I don't like you to see violent movies, Barbara." Mrs. Dapple's arms were crossed in front of her.

"Mom, it's got a PG rating. All the kids are seeing it."

Mrs. Dapple shook her head. "I don't know why they don't make good monster movies anymore. Horror films used to have artistic merit."

Barbara raised her eyes toward the ceiling.

"Well," Mrs. Dapple went on, "I suppose you can see it if it's a PG. But Margaret is awfully young for this kind of thing."

"She certainly is. Childhood traumas can scar you for life," Barbara informed her mother.

"A rotten sister could scar you worse!" Margaret put in. "Besides, I don't have to look. I can sit with my eyes closed."

The two sisters stood facing their mother waiting for her decision.

"Margaret," Mrs. Dapple said, "I'm sorry. Daddy and I will take you to the movies on Saturday, and Barbara will go with her friends today. There's a new comedy opening which I hear is very good.

Mrs. Dapple turned to Barbara. "And in the future, Barbara, don't make promises you don't intend to keep!"

Total victory for Barbara. That's all this was. Margaret flopped down onto a kitchen chair. "It's not fair. Why does Barbara get her way? I want to go with her!"

"Well, you can't. So forget it!" Barbara began buttoning her sweater.

"That's enough, Barbara. If you're going to the movies, I suggest you leave right now. And don't be late for dinner."

"I was just leaving." And with a victorious look at Margaret, Barbara put on her jacket and walked out the door.

☆ **2** ☆

Margaret was not finished pleading her case. She was secretly glad that her mother had saved her from sitting through a gruesome movie, and going with her parents on Saturday was not such a bad deal. But there was a principle at stake here. She followed her mother as she walked to the hall closet with her coat and Margaret's jacket slung over her arm.

"I really wanted to go to the movies today. Nobody around here keeps a promise."

Her mother placed her own coat on a large wooden hanger and Margaret's jacket on a smaller wire one. "If I recall correctly, you're not so good at keeping promises yourself."

Margaret hated that tone of voice. It meant her mother was about to come up with a good point.

Mrs. Dapple headed back toward the kitchen with Margaret still at her heels. "Don't you have a book report to write for tomorrow? And didn't you promise not to write compositions at the last minute anymore?"

If I did, it was a stupid promise, Margaret thought to herself.

"Your last grade could have been better. Why don't you go and finish your assignment? I'll read it over when you're done."

"*Now?* You want me to do my homework *now?*" Margaret could not believe her ears. Didn't her mother realize the injustice that had been done to her? She certainly was not going to do homework while Barbara was enjoying herself at the movies. That was too much!

"Margaret, do your report now. Get it over with. Then you can watch TV tonight."

Since Margaret had been expecting to watch TV anyway, this didn't seem like such a hot deal. "Can I stay up an extra hour?" she asked, negotiating for better terms.

"Okay, forty-five minutes. But only if you do your homework now."

Margaret ran off to her room. An extra forty-five minutes of TV was something of a victory. Especially from a mother who thought TV was for morons.

"And don't be sloppy!" her mother called after her. "Think before you write."

Margaret ignored these remarks. Her mother was always saying things like that. It was probably because she was a teacher. Too bad she acted like one at home.

Margaret went into her room and flopped on the bed. She picked up a stack of loose-leaf paper and her favorite pen. It wrote in four different colors, and she could pick the one she wanted just by pressing one button. Margaret decided to click down the green ink. Everyone in the class had been told to read a book about a country in South America and then do a book report. Margaret had picked Peru because she already knew the capital was Lima. She figured that gave her a headstart. The book she had read was called *The Incas of Peru*. It was an okay book with good pictures, but what was she supposed to say about it? She used her standard opening for all book reports: "I found this book very interesting." Now what? She had nothing else to say. She began drawing triangles and coloring them in black. She hated writing book reports. How did teachers expect you to like to read if you always had to write a book report? The page began to fill up with her scribbles. No new information about the Incas or Peru was appearing. I need another sentence, Margaret goaded herself.

"It tells you important things about Peru," Margaret wrote slowly. Okay. That was two lines. She probably needed a million more. This was going to be some job! Margaret threw down her pen. She went to her door and opened it a crack.

She could hear her mother talking on the telephone. It was safe. She went to her desk and picked up another book. It was a Nancy Drew mystery called *The Hidden Staircase*. Margaret loved all the Nancy Drew stories. When she read them she was no longer baby Margaret Dapple, sitting in a narrow rectangular room, with a highrise bed that was supposed to look like a couch, a brown shelf stuffed with books, a dresser, and a broken record player. She was Margaret Dapple, close friend of Nancy Drew, accompanying

her to exotic places to solve the most puzzling mysteries.

Margaret pushed her papers aside and snuggled into a corner of her bed. She turned to the page with the turned-down corner. "I really should use bookmarks," she reprimanded herself. She was up to page ninety. That was halfway through the book. Assuming her favorite reading position—one leg drawn to her chest and the other crossed over it, book propped on her stomach—Margaret settled down. And as she read the first sentence, she thought to herself, Now *this* is a good book!

☆ 3 ☆

"Margaret!"

Margaret was startled by her mother's shrill voice. Engrossed in her book, she was watching Nancy pay a visit on the suspected criminal and hoping she'd come out alive.

"Margaret!" her mother shouted impatiently. "Telephone!"

"Who is it?" Margaret yelled, annoyed at the interruption.

"Tamara."

"Okay. I'll be right there." Reluctantly turning the book face down on the bed, Margaret went to the telephone. "Hi, Tamara."

"Margaret, are you sitting down?" Tamara sounded breathless. "I've got something sensational to tell you!"

"Oh? What is it?" asked Margaret, still with Nancy.

"This is *super, super* news. Honestly, Margaret, you are going to die!"

Tamara was beside herself with excitement. Margaret could hear her jumping up and down. What was going on? "Well, tell me already!"

"Are you ready?"

"I'm ready! I'm ready! Tell me!"

"Naomi just called me. She and Stephen went to the park together this afternoon. They went *all alone*. They went down to the steps by the playground and sat together on the rocks."

"So what? We always go to the park."

"Margaret! I'm not finished! They held hands and then . . . THEY KISSED!"

Margaret was dazed. Naomi kissed a boy. A boy kissed Naomi. What was there to say? A girl in her class had kissed a boy. Margaret knew that some of the girls in Class 6-3 were kissing boys, but everyone in her class thought it was awful. At least she thought it was.

Margaret's heart was beating quickly. She envisioned Stephen's arms around Naomi, clasping her to him, their eyes tightly shut, their kiss long. Just like on television. It was too horrible to think about. But Margaret couldn't stop dwelling on the image she had conjured up. She was fascinated. How did people kiss with their eyes closed? How did their lips meet? What happened to their teeth? What did it feel like? Was it different from when your family kissed you? It must be. Why else the big fuss? How did Naomi feel? Did she giggle? Margaret would have. What did Naomi do afterwards? Probably went home and brushed her teeth. Why was Tamara so excited about this anyway? Big deal! But Margaret's heart was pounding and her stomach was jumping. Margaret knew she was excited too.

"Isn't that something, Margaret?" squealed Tamara.

"Are you sure about this?" Margaret asked shakily.

"Am I sure? Of course I'm sure! Naomi told me *everything*. They're in love. They're even going on a date to the movies this Saturday. I wonder if they'll kiss in the movies!"

"*This* Saturday?" Margaret hoped she had heard wrong.

"Saturday afternoon, I guess. I don't think Naomi's mother will let her go out with Stephen at night."

Oh no! Margaret's mind was reeling. What if Naomi and Stephen were going to the same movie she was going to with her parents? She'd die if she saw them there. They'd be on a *date*, and she'd be sitting there with her mother and father. They'd think she was such a baby! This was all Barbara's fault. Why hadn't she taken her to the movies today like she'd promised? Margaret would kill her. But first she would tell her parents she wasn't going with them on Saturday.

Tamara was still talking. "I wish Adam would ask me for a date. He's always staring at me. Do you think he likes me?"

Somewhere in her mind Margaret knew somebody had asked her a question, but she couldn't remember what it was. She was still thinking about Naomi and Stephen, dating, kissing, and showing up at the movies Saturday afternoon.

"Well, do you, Margaret? Do you think Adam likes me?"

"He's always staring at you."

"I know that, Margaret! I just told you! Are you there?"

"Sure I am."

"Well, act like it, please!" Tamara sounded exasperated. "Is there anyone you'd like to go out with?"

"No. I think the boys in our class are pretty stupid," Margaret managed to mumble.

"They are pretty ugly," Tamara acknowledged. "Except Adam."

"I have to go now," Margaret cut in. "I was working on my book report when you called, and I promised to finish it before dinner."

"The book report! Oh no! Thanks for reminding me! I forgot all about it!" Tamara was frantic. "I have a gigantic book on Uruguay. And I haven't even looked at it! I'm sorry, Margaret, but I have to go. See you tomorrow. Bye!"

"Bye." Margaret put the receiver down. She went back to her room, climbed back on her bed, and picked up Nancy Drew. Her eyes were reading, but her mind wasn't. It was as if the words kept dancing behind her forehead but couldn't get further back. Talking to Tamara had really upset her. Was it running into Naomi and Stephen at the movies? That was part of it. What did Stephen see in dumb Naomi anyway? Margaret had never liked her very much. Naomi could be your best friend one day and ignore you the next. And she was bossy too. She had to be the leader in everything. But there was something else too. Something much worse was bothering Margaret. She had lied to Tamara. Not just the part about hanging up to work on her book report. It was a much bigger lie. She did like somebody, but she had never told a soul. And she never would. Most of the boys in the class were ugly and stupid. But there was one who wasn't. He was the one Margaret prayed would sit next to her in assembly, and he was the one Margaret wanted to go out with. Stephen.

☆ **4** ☆

"Hi, Maggie Mae! How're you doing?" Barbara poked her head into Margaret's room. "Supper will be ready soon." Margaret was so absorbed in grappling with Tamara's news, she hadn't even heard Barbara come home. But she was glad to see her now.

"How was the movie?"

"Great. You would have hated it. The beginning was a little boring, but then it got real good." Barbara sat down on Margaret's bed. "I'm sure the movie you'll be seeing is good, too."

"Actually, I don't think I'm going Saturday." Margaret tried to sound casual. "I'm sick of movies."

"MAR-GA-RET!" Barbara's eyes were so wide they almost hid her forehead. "You were dying to go today. I always knew you were a little touched, but this is *ridiculous!* I think you're truly losing your mind," Barbara said.

"I have better things to do on Saturday."

"Like what?" said Barbara, implying in that way of hers that nothing Margaret had to do could be so important.

"Like going to the library."

Barbara eyed Margaret suspiciously. "Suit yourself, toots." she said, her attention now drawn to the Nancy Drew book lying on the bed. "I read this once. It was good. Did you get to the scary part yet?"

"Lots of it is scary." Margaret scarcely glanced at the book.

Barbara studied Margaret again. "What's the matter, Marg? You're acting crazier than usual. Did you have another fight with Mom?"

"No, it's not that." Margaret dragged the words out slowly, hoping her sister would force her to tell.

"Then what is it? I'm not leaving till I know!"

Oh good! Now she had no choice. Margaret wrapped her arms around her clown pajama bag and hugged it to her stomach. "I don't think I know much about life," Margaret began haltingly.

For a second Barbara looked as though she might agree. Then her expression changed and she began to remind Margaret of a psychologist she'd seen on TV. "What makes you say that?" Barbara asked in a soothing voice.

"Tamara told me some very shocking things about Naomi today."

"Like what?" Barbara asked, still maintaining her open, "you-can-trust-me" style.

"I don't know if I should tell anybody. It may be a secret."

"I'm not just anybody. I'm your sister! You can tell me anything!"

"Promise you won't tell a soul?"

"My lips are sealed," said Barbara, lifting an imaginary key to her lips and locking them.

Margaret took a deep breath, hugged her knees, and spilled out her story, all about Naomi and Stephen and the park, and the kiss, and the date, and the movies on Saturday, and even her own love for Stephen.

"Wow!" Barbara's mouth hung open. "They actually kissed?"

Margaret was pleased to see that even sophisticated Barbara was rattled by this news.

"These kids today are really something," Barbara went on. "And you really like Stephen?"

Margaret nodded yes, her eyes watery.

"And he likes Naomi?"

Margaret nodded again.

"This is a low ego time for you."

Margaret didn't know what that meant, but for once Barbara's psychology sounded right.

"She kissed him, huh?"

"Yes," Margaret said in a small voice.

"Well, this is quite a situation," Barbara said. "I think I saw a movie like this once."

"How did it end?"

"I don't remember. I think somebody committed suicide."

"That's great," Margaret sighed.

"Oh don't worry!" Barbara reassured her. "With close attention to the rules which govern human behavior and some clever strategies everything will be all right."

"I don't have any clever strategies. Do you?"

"Not yet. But don't worry." Barbara placed an arm around Margaret's shoulders. "We'll think of something."

☆ 5 ☆

At supper that evening Margaret was extremely quiet. Mr. Dapple did his best to cheer her by telling what he considered some of his best jokes.

"What did one tonsil say to the other tonsil?" Mr. Dapple asked as he passed the carrots.

Nobody answered.

"Get dressed. The doctor's taking us out tonight!" Mr. Dapple shook with laughter.

"Oh, Daddy—that's awful!" Barbara moaned, dumping ketchup on her meat. "I have a better one. Why is it good to play cards in a cemetery?"

Nobody knew.

"Because you can always dig up an extra player!"

Barbara and her parents laughed. But Margaret was silent. She busied herself rearranging the food on her plate into neat little piles which she then neglected to eat. Margaret knew this was a form of torment for her mother who couldn't stand it when she or Barbara didn't eat. Barbara, in an effort to draw attention away from her sister, chatted brightly about the film she had seen, informing her parents that if her career as a psychologist didn't work out, she would be happy to settle for movie stardom. But Barbara could not help glancing over to Margaret, who would meet Barbara's eyes, turn deep red and look away. Finally Mr. Dapple raised an eyebrow and looked questioningly at Mrs. Dapple. He turned to Margaret.

"So," Mr. Dapple began in a breezy voice, "what did you do today, Maggie?"

"Nothing," Margaret answered, pushing all her potatoes over to one side of the plate.

"Anything new happen in school?" Mr. Dapple tried again.

"No." Margaret drew a sharp dividing line between her potatoes and carrots and positioned the carrots over to the opposite side of the plate.

"How's math coming along?"

"Fine," Margaret answered, mashing her potatoes.

Mrs. Dapple took over. "How's Tamara?"

Margaret could feel her cheeks burn instantly. Why did her mother always ask the right questions?

"She's okay."

"You certainly had quite a long chat with her today," her mother commented as she tossed the salad. Margaret, who felt a little tossed about herself, wished her mother would change the subject. "Did she have anything interesting to say?" Mrs. Dapple continued, blithely ignoring Margaret's reluctance to talk.

"No," Margaret said, purposely dropping her fork on the floor to avoid further questioning. She crawled under the table to retrieve her fork, which was now lying next to her mother's foot. Everybody's legs seemed so long, her father's feet enormous. If only she could crawl between everybody's legs and sneak out of the kitchen!

Margaret climbed back into her seat. Her little trick had worked. Her mother had forgotten all about Margaret and Tamara and was now discussing a lecture she had attended on new methods of education. She expressed her certainty that Margaret's school hadn't had a new teaching idea since 1902, an issue she'd be sure to raise at the next PTA meeting. Barbara cheerfully allowed how this was probably why Margaret was so dumb, but Mrs. Dapple was quick to remind Barbara that her junior high school was hardly a model educational institution either. This was the perfect opportunity for Margaret to make her escape.

"I better go finish my book report now." She got up from the table.

"You didn't finish it yet? A little less talk on the telephone would mean a lot more work!"

"It's a very hard book with big words, Mom," Margaret offered, certain that somehow her mother knew she had been reading Nancy Drew instead of working.

"Maybe Barbara can help you," Mr. Dapple volunteered.

Barbara, who had been planning to listen to records all evening, was not pleased. "I have a lot of algebra to do."

"You're an A student in algebra." Mr. Dapple waved his fork in the air. "Why don't you help your sister?"

"I really don't want to do her homework."

"Barbara, don't be so selfish," her father persisted.

"She certainly is your favorite!" Barbara's knife clattered on her plate. "As usual, I'm expected to bear all the burdens!" But one look at Margaret's pained expression aroused Barbara's sympathies.

"Okay, okay. I'll help her. Come on, Margaret. Let's go."

"Girls, you haven't eaten dessert yet," Mrs. Dapple said.

"We'll take it to my room and eat it while I do my homework." Margaret wanted to avoid any argument that might keep her in the kitchen.

"All right. It's in the refrigerator."

They each took out a serving of chocolate pudding with whipped cream. Margaret, who had not had the slightest appetite all through dinner, immediately felt hungry at the sight of something sweet.

"See you later." Margaret quickly exited from the kitchen with Barbara behind her.

"Don't get any food on your homework!" a voice called after them.

Mother, the teacher, had struck again!

☆ 6 ☆

"Okay, Margaret. Let's see this book." Barbara got right down to business. No moping around with her! Margaret handed it over.

"Oh, this does look boring," Barbara said, looking at the cover. "What have you written so far?"

Margaret shoved over her two-sentence book report.

"At this rate we'll be here all night!" Barbara opened the book. "Margaret, there are some perfectly good sentences right here on the book jacket. Copy them!"

Margaret looked doubtful. She had always been tempted to copy right off the book jacket, and once in a while she'd even used a few words. But she was always afraid her teacher would go to the library and get out the book she had read to check if she had copied.

"What if Mrs. Kopelman goes to the library to see if I copied?"

"Are you for real? She doesn't have the time to check on everybody's book report. Grow up!" Barbara pointed again to the inside flap of the book. "Use these sentences here."

She may not have time to check on *everybody's* book report, Margaret thought nervously, but she just might have the time to check on mine! What if she got caught? She might be expelled.

"Those sentences sound a little too grown-up for me," Margaret insisted.

"You're not supposed to use them word for word. That's cheating. Anyway, the teacher can always tell. You have to change them a little."

Margaret was confused. She didn't know what was right anymore. But she certainly knew she wanted to get this report finished, and Barbara seemed to know how to do it.

"Now this is a great sentence." Barbara read from the flap:

"This uniquely informative, yet easy-to-read book offers a detailed discussion of the intricate economic system of the Incas."

"I don't understand that," Margaret whined.

Barbara sighed. "Just write, 'This is a good book that tells how the Incas earned a living.'"

Barbara sure was good at writing book reports. Margaret carefully wrote down Barbara's words. She should have used her before.

"Here's another great sentence. Listen:

"Young readers will delight at Mr. Christopher's deft handling of the history of the ancient Incas."

"What does that mean?" Margaret was quite baffled. "I don't remember reading that the Incas couldn't hear."

"DEFT, stupid! Not deaf! That means he does it well. Give me a break." Barbara sighed. "Put down, 'The author does a good job of explaining the history of the Incas.' "

"This is really easy." Margaret was delighted. "I only need a few more sentences." She looked up at Barbara expectantly. "What should I say?"

"Honestly, Margaret, I can't write the whole thing for you!"

Margaret was not exactly sure why she couldn't, but it seemed better not to push the issue.

"Maybe I could talk about the end of the empire."

"That's good. Then the teacher will know you read the whole book."

Margaret wrote down a sentence about how the Spaniards took the Incas' gold and killed their emperor.

"Now what should I write?"

"What else did you like?"

"I liked the pictures," Margaret offered. "There were pictures of old ruins and caves where they buried people."

"So say something about them."

Margaret quickly wrote down a sentence about the book's illustrations.

"Now you only need a summary sentence," Barbara prompted.

"Mrs. Kopelman always likes us to give our opinion about the book."

"Terrific. That's easy."

Margaret was tremendously impressed with her sister's casual attitude towards book reports. They had always seemed so difficult to her.

"I'll write that I recommend this book to anybody who wants to learn something about ancient Peru. It's excellent."

"Perfect!" Barbara exclaimed.

"Now all I have to do is copy this over neatly and draw a cover for the report. I might even be able to see some TV!"

"I guess I'll go listen to my records now and do my math."

"Thanks a million, Barbara." Margaret looked up at her sister standing in the doorway. "You're the best sister in the whole world."

"It really wasn't so bad," Barbara smiled. "Writing book reports is a lot easier than algebra!"

Margaret smiled back and silently resolved to find a junior high school that did not require algebra.

As soon as Barbara had gone, Margaret settled down to rewrite her book report. She spread her papers on the floor and picked out some construction paper to use for the cover. Eyeing her clock, she noticed it was already 8:30. How much longer would her mother let her stay up? When would she get to watch TV? Margaret gathered all her papers, her pens and her crayons and headed for the living room. "Copying doesn't require much concentration," she said to herself. "I can rewrite this and watch TV at the same time!"

When Margaret entered the living room, her mother was sitting on the couch correcting a batch of her students' papers. Her father was stretched out in his reclining chair. The TV was already on. A beautiful woman was singing and four men were dancing around her. Margaret plopped her papers down on the floor in front of the TV.

"What are you doing?" Mrs. Dapple looked up from her papers.

"I'm going to recopy my book report."

"Here? With the TV on? Don't you think you should be doing that in your room? You can't concentrate with the television on."

"Yes, I can. I can concentrate anywhere. Anyway, you're marking papers with the TV on."

Mrs. Dapple tried to fight a smile. "I've had years of practice at doing two things at once. It's going to be a long time before you're as good at it as I am!"

Margaret made a face.

"Hurry up and finish your work. You have to go to bed soon. I'll check it when it's done."

What a pain her mother was! With her hand on her pen, but her eyes on the screen, Margaret settled down to watch the program. The dancing men had disappeared, and the woman was now joined by another woman and a man. The three of them were sitting on stools and singing. But Margaret didn't hear them anymore. As she stared at the two female singers, her mind wandered. She wondered if they both loved that man. Did he love one of them more than the other?

Margaret thought about her own unhappy situation with Naomi and Stephen. Stephen didn't love her. He didn't even know she was alive. But what was worse, by Saturday he *would* know she was alive, because he would also know she was a big baby who was not ready to be his girlfriend. Margaret glanced down at her book report. It was a good thing it only had to be recopied. She couldn't even remember the name of the book.

☆ 7 ☆

Margaret walked into Room 402 of P.S. 187 and sat next to Tamara. Margaret had the first seat in Row 3 and Tamara had the first seat in Row 2. Mrs. Kopelman sat the shorter kids in the front so they wouldn't be stuck behind somebody's big head. Margaret noticed immediately that Tamara was wearing another new outfit. She had on a brown, gray and beige plaid skirt with a beige long-sleeved sweater that had three wooden buttons on the shoulder. Tamara said her father was in "wholesale" and that was why she always wore the nicest clothes. Margaret looked over to Stephen, as she always did, sitting in the last seat of Row 1 near the paper closet. He was busy sticking reinforcements on his loose-leaf papers and didn't seem to notice Margaret. It was funny. Kissing a girl didn't make him look any different. Yet of all the mornings she admired him, today he seemed the handsomest. Mrs. Kopelman began taking attendance, and Tamara and Margaret started whispering about their book reports.

"Adam Astor," Mrs. Kopelman began the roll call.

"Here."

"Matthew Berger."

"Here."

"Wendy Carey."

"Here."

"Margaret Dapple."

Margaret was still talking to Tamara.

"Margaret Dapple," Mrs. Kopelman repeated loudly.

"Oh. Here!"

Everyone began laughing. Margaret could feel her cheeks burning. Stephen must think she was such a fool!

"Max Elliot," Mrs. Kopelman continued.

"Here."

"Dawn Ellison."

"Here."

"Naomi Finer. . . . Naomi Finer," Mrs. Kopelman looked up from her roll book.

There was no answer. Margaret scanned the classroom along with Mrs. Kopelman. It was true! Naomi was absent. Maybe she was sick. How wonderful! Margaret checked herself for having such bad thoughts about somebody. But still, if Naomi was sick—and she didn't have to be very sick, a bad cold would do—she wouldn't be able to go to the movies on Saturday. And then she wouldn't be able to see Stephen. That would solve all of Margaret's problems!

"Ralph Frank." Mrs. Kopelman was still calling the roll. The boy with two first names was present.

"Tamara," Margaret whispered to her friend, "what's the matter with Naomi?"

"I don't know. I spoke to her yesterday, and she didn't say she'd be absent. Maybe she didn't do her book report and decided to stay home."

"Her mother would never let her stay home for that," Margaret replied. Anyway, *her* mother wouldn't. It could be, Margaret mused, that Naomi's mother was punishing her for kissing Stephen. That made more sense. At this very minute, Naomi could be home being yelled at by her mother. Margaret hoped she was getting it good.

"Do you think my book report is long enough?" Tamara shoved her book report over to Margaret.

"Mine's not any longer," Margaret offered.

"Actually, yours looks a little short to me."

Some comfort Tamara was.

"Margaret and Tamara! I hate to interrupt your apparently engrossing conversation, but we're doing math now!"

Mrs. Kopelman had her arms folded in front of her, and was glaring at both of them. She just loved using big words. "Mrs. Dictionary," Margaret called her. Margaret faced the blackboard, took out her loose leaf, and turned to the math section. She began copying the division examples on the board.

"Naomi is absent! Naomi is absent!" Margaret was humming to herself. What good news. Of course, today was Friday, and she might get well by tomorrow. But then again, she might not! Margaret tackled her math with new energy. This was going to be a great day!

"Let's see. 480 divided by 25." Margaret could see Tamara out of the corner of her eye counting on her fingers under her desk. Mrs. Kopelman hated finger counting. She was so strict sometimes. Over to her left, Margaret could see Max Elliot showing off his answer to Mrs. Kopelman. As usual, he was the first one done, and Mrs. Kopelman praised him loudly.

"Class, Max has already completed the first example perfectly. Put number one on the board," she said to a beaming Max.

People like Max always ruined it for the rest of the class, Margaret observed. Why couldn't he have given everyone else just five more minutes? He probably had a calculator in his pocket. But much as Margaret would have liked to believe that, she knew it wasn't true. Max had been in her class since second grade, and he was simply a math genius. He did once let Margaret see his homework and copy an example she hadn't done, so he wasn't all bad. There he was now, showing the class how he had computed 25 into 480. Max's answer was "19 5/25 or 19 1/5." Margaret looked at her paper. She had "18 5/25." She must have done something wrong. Certainly Max hadn't.

"Who has the answer to the second problem?" Mrs. Kopelman looked around the class. Julie Marshall was leaning all the way forward in her seat. She was waving her hand wildly and making noises as if she had a stomach ache.

"Ooooo—Pick me! Pick me! Please Mrs. Kopleman!" Her two braids, which were somehow never the same length, were bobbing up and down. Margaret and Tamara exchanged sickened looks.

"All right, Julie. Go to the board."

As Julie scratched her calculations on the blackboard, Margaret wrote furiously, trying to get the answer to 735 divided by 60. Tamara was leaning over to look at Margaret's paper. Tamara's strength was multiplication, not long division. Although she could do it when she had to, it took her a long time, and she'd just as soon use Margaret's answer as figure out her own. This was a snap. "12 15/60 or 12 1/4." Margaret shoved her paper over toward Tamara so she could see. Margaret put her pencil down and looked at the board. Yes, Julie had the same answer. She was right! Mrs. Kopelman was standing next to Margaret. She smiled at her as she put a check next to her answer.

Margaret eagerly set about solving the other problems on the blackboard. 15 into 325 was 21 2/3; 18 into 620 was 34 4/9; and 28 into 1,250 was 44 9/14. The answers came pouring out.

My brain is certainly working today, Margaret marveled. I bet I could even learn algebra!

Tamara kept poking Margaret for help, and Margaret gladly showed her how to work out the problems. Even Tamara was beginning to catch on.

"Naomi. How nice to see you." Mrs. Kopelman's voice came floating up from the back of the sixth row. "We all thought you were sick."

Margaret's pencil fell from her hand. There stood Naomi holding out her late pass.

"Take your seat, Naomi. We're finishing a math drill."

Naomi sauntered up the fourth row to her seat like a princess walking to her throne. Margaret's eyes followed her. Naomi never bumped into people's desks and knocked their pencil cases off, like Margaret did. No wonder Stephen liked her. Was he watching her? Yes, he was. Naomi was definitely not sick. She was in perfect health. She'd be at that movie tomorrow. Margaret was miserable. Why couldn't anything work for her? Why couldn't Naomi have been sick for a few days? Margaret was no longer interested in math. Why couldn't Naomi have been kidnapped? The class was filing out the door before Margaret realized that Mrs. Kopelman had announced recess. She got up and trudged to the end of the line. Margaret was in no mood for punch ball, dodge ball, jump rope or anything. How could she have been so happy two hours ago? It seemed like two years ago.

This was going to be a terrible day.

☆ 8 ☆

Somehow Margaret managed to get through the rest of Friday. It wasn't easy. The day was mostly a blur. All Margaret could think about was her broken heart and her rotten luck. If it had been anyone else, Naomi would be dead by now. But did Margaret ever have that kind of luck? Not her! Naomi was back in school, and Stephen still liked her. Margaret had noticed them staring at each other in class, and she had even seen Naomi pass Stephen a note. It probably said, "I love you." Why hadn't that blind Mrs. Kopelman seen her doing it? She caught Margaret every time she so much as whispered to Tamara! It was obvious that Mrs. Kopelman liked Naomi. Teachers had no taste. Margaret was certain that even her own mother had a favorite in her class. She could only hope her mother wasn't as easily fooled as Mrs. Kopelman.

When Margaret came home from school, Barbara was in the kitchen preparing dinner.

"What's with you? You look awful!" Barbara was slicing carrots and eating most of them.

Margaret grabbed a piece of carrot and bit into it. "Don't ask. My life is over."

"Too bad. You never even got big enough for me to wear your clothes," Barbara laughed.

"Just leave me alone!" Margaret snapped.

"Well, excuse me! What happened? Are Naomi and Stephen married?" Barbara began laughing again.

Oh, she was horrible! Just wait till her life was crumbling.

"Help me with dinner," Barbara washed off another carrot. "Mom is at a school board meeting and Daddy is picking her up on his way home from work. We're supposed to make dinner."

"You mean Mommy isn't home?" Margaret was desperate. If only her mother were home, she'd feel a little better. Margaret stuffed a chocolate bar into her mouth.

"Start rinsing the lettuce." Barbara handed her a colander. "Cinderella is not doing everything. And don't eat so much candy. I'm going to tell Mommy!"

Margaret remained fixed to her spot. "The brown leaves make me sick. Let me do something else."

"Do you know how to peel potatoes?"

"No," Margaret muttered.

"Don't you do anything around here? Boy are you spoiled! When I was your age, I always helped Mom with supper." Barbara took a vegetable peeler out of a drawer. "Well, start learning! Here's a peeler."

Margaret felt tears welling. Hadn't her day been bad enough? Did she have to come home to this? Where was her mother anyway? Tamara never *once* made dinner in her whole life. Nothing ever went right for Margaret. "Just leave me alone," she said.

"Margaret, start helping. I've got a lot to do."

"Do it yourself, big shot."

"I'm gonna knock you out, squirt! Start helping!"

"I'm not going to!" Margaret cried. "Make me!" she darted out of the kitchen with Barbara running after her.

"Get back here and help!" Barbara shouted.

"What's going on here?" Mr. Dapple's voice came booming from the hallway. "This is some welcome home!"

Margaret ran into her father's arms. "Barbara's going to kill me. She's been bossing me around all afternoon!"

"Go ahead, baby. Run to Daddy!"

"Barbara! Margaret! Be quiet! Both of you!" Mrs. Dapple hung up her coat in the hall closet. "I'm really in no mood for this. Is dinner almost ready?"

Mrs. Dapple walked into the kitchen, with Margaret right behind.

"Mom, everything is terrible," Margaret wailed.

"Can't you kids get anything done? Nothing is ready!" Mrs. Dapple looked around the kitchen.

"Ma! Listen to me!"

"Did you say something, Margaret? I'm sorry. What's the matter?" Mrs. Dapple began peeling potatoes. Margaret watched as her mother methodically stripped each potato of its skin. Could she confide in her mother? Maybe. Sometimes her mother had good ideas.

"I had such a terrible day, and I—"

Mr. Dapple came into the kitchen and began preparing the salad. She certainly couldn't tell her mother about Stephen and Naomi now that her father was here. It was just too embarrassing.

"Margaret, everything will be all right. We'll have a nice dinner and maybe we'll all play Scrabble later."

"Not me, gang." Barbara was standing at the open refrigerator eating cheese. "I'm going out."

"Where are you going?" Mrs. Dapple began boiling a large pot of water.

"Jessica is going to pierce an extra hole in Lisa's right ear. I'm going over to watch."

"Shouldn't Lisa have a doctor do it?"

"Mom!" Barbara groaned. "Jessica has done

this a thousand times! She's better than a doctor!''

"The whole thing sounds gruesome to me," Mr. Dapple commented.

Mrs. Dapple looked up from setting the table. "You just make sure she doesn't touch your ears. Is that clear?"

"All right!" Barbara let the refrigerator door slam shut.

"Well, Margaret," Mrs. Dapple set a napkin by each plate, "you, Daddy, and I will have a nice evening by ourselves. And tomorrow will be fine. We're all going to the movies. You'll have a great time." Margaret looked at her parents busily setting the table and a new wave of despair hit her.

Yeah, she thought. A great time.

☆ 9 ☆

"Hurry up, Margaret. It's 1:30. What's taking you so long?"

"I can't find my shoes, Ma. I've looked everywhere."

"I'm sure they're in your closet."

"I looked there."

"Look under your bed. Everything's usually there. And hurry up! We only have forty-five minutes to get to the movie theater."

Margaret was stalling. If she could just waste enough time, maybe she wouldn't have to go. Her father hated to enter a theater once the movie had already started. Poking under her bed, Margaret found her shoes. She also found two comic books she'd been looking for since last week. This seemed like a good time to read them. Margaret sat on her bed and opened "Betty and Veronica."

"Margaret! Daddy is getting the car. Move it!"

"I don't have my shoes on yet."

"Well, put them on," her mother called impatiently.

Margaret put down the comic book and put on her shoes. They were so ugly. Why did her mother always make her wear the creepiest shoes? Tamara had beautiful shoes, but Margaret's mother said those kinds weren't good for your feet. Mrs. Dapple insisted that children should wear good sturdy shoes so that their feet would develop properly. Tamara's feet looked just fine to Margaret. She was the best runner in the class. Junky shoes hadn't seemed to hurt her.

Naomi will probably be wearing high heels. Margaret thought to herself. Oh, I look like such a baby! Please, God, don't make me see Naomi and Stephen at the movies! If you don't, I'll never fight with Barbara again. I promise!

"Margaret, come on! We're leaving right now!"

Margaret came out of her room and met her mother at the front door.

"What's the matter with you? A few days ago you couldn't wait to go to the movies. I can't understand you!" Fortunately, Mrs. Dapple was in too much of a hurry to wait for Margaret's explanation, and she rushed her out the door.

As soon as they neared the theater, Mr. Dapple began to grumble. "Look at those lines! I knew we should have left earlier."

Mr. Dapple let Margaret and her mother out of the car to buy tickets while he went to park.

"This movie certainly is popular," Mrs. Dapple observed as Margaret and she passed by the long line of waiting people. But all Margaret could think of was that Naomi and Stephen might be on that very line watching her arrive with her mother. She stared straight ahead and ran to the end. After a few minutes, Margaret saw her father coming up the street. He looked mad.

"This city is impossible. Do you know what it just cost me to park?"

I wish he wouldn't talk so loudly, Margaret thought to herself. What if Naomi recognized his voice?

"And then, the guy made me feel lucky to be able to park at all!"

Daddy, be quiet! Didn't he know his voice was an announcement to everyone that said, "I'm Margaret's father. She's here with me and not a boy. She's my baby"?

With her eyes glued to the ground, Margaret entered the theater with her parents. There were three seats in the rear of the center section. Although Margaret and her father usually liked to sit up close, Margaret had no interest in walking down the aisle to find better seats. She was not going to parade herself in front of everyone in the theater. And everyone meant Naomi and Stephen.

"Let's take these seats here," Margaret told her father who was still looking around. "They're okay."

Mrs. Dapple, Mr. Dapple, and Margaret moved into the row, carefully stepping over people's feet and pocketbooks. Her parents motioned for Margaret to sit down. Usually Margaret's favorite spot was next to her father. But not today. She sat herself on her mother's right and prayed for the lights to go out.

"We still have a couple of minutes. Let's hit the candy counter." Her father extended his hand to Margaret.

This was usually the best part of going to the movies with her parents. Her father always let her buy all the junk she wanted. But today Margaret wasn't interested. She was safe just where she was. If she walked out to the candy counter, she might bump into Naomi and Stephen. She couldn't bear that. She and her *daddy* buying candy? No way! The idea made Margaret sweat.

"I don't really want anything, Daddy. I'm not hungry."

"Not hungry for sweets? I can't believe it!"

"Don't push it, Alan," her mother muttered. "At least she won't rot her teeth."

Margaret crouched down in her seat. Why didn't this stupid movie begin already? The darkness would be her protection.

At last the lights dimmed and the curtain parted. Soon the theater was totally dark except for the light from the screen. Margaret began to relax. She sat up and looked around. Maybe she could spot Naomi and Stephen. Occasional reflections of light hit the audience and Margaret seized these moments to try and find them.

Oh no! There they were! Naomi and Stephen huddled together. Kissing! Margaret was sick. Look at them! He's touching her neck! She's nibbling his ear! I can't stand this! Margaret's head was swimming. What are they doing now? I can't watch! Margaret kept watching. The girl put her arm around the boy and looked behind her, still nuzzling his neck. Margaret was going to collapse. Wait! That's not Naomi. That lady is old! She looks thirty! Margaret was filled with relief. Thank God it wasn't Naomi. What an awful thing she had witnessed!

"Margaret, isn't that funny?" Her mother was nudging her.

Margaret was still eyeing the couple she had taken for Naomi and Stephen.

"Yes, Mom. It's really funny." But Margaret wasn't laughing. The rest of the movie was torture for her. She kept trying to locate Naomi and Stephen and often repeated her first mistake.

Margaret had never realized how many girls looked like Naomi! After what seemed like ten hours, the credits rolled and the lights came on. So far so good. No Naomi and Stephen. Margaret jumped up and prepared to rush out of the theater before her luck changed. Fortunately she was sitting in the back. People were already coming up the aisles on their way out.

"Margaret! Look, it's Naomi!" Mrs. Dapple was pointing over to the right side of the theater.

Oh, God, no! Where? "I don't see her."

Margaret tried to push past her father and get to the exit.

Mrs. Dapple was waving. "Mrs. Finer! Mrs. Finer! Hi!"

Mrs. Finer? What was her mother talking about?

Margaret looked around. There was Mrs. Finer walking up the aisle. Her arms were around Naomi and Stephen. Naomi and Stephen! Right in front of her! With Naomi's mother!

Margaret gawked at them. Naomi was at the movies with her date and her *mother!* Margaret felt light-headed. This was a laugh! What a riot! Wait till she told Tamara.

Margaret's mother started chatting with Mrs. Finer. They told each other how well they looked and how they must get together soon. Margaret just stared at Naomi who stared at the red exit sign at the back of the theater. Stephen just stared at the floor.

Margaret could not believe this. Naomi was just a baby too! Maybe even more of a baby. Margaret gathered up her courage and looked Stephen squarely in the face. Somehow he didn't look as handsome today. But before she had time to figure out why, Naomi, Mrs. Finer, and Stephen were gone, and Margaret was filing out of the exit of the theater with her parents.

Her worst fears had come true. She had bumped into Naomi and Stephen at the movies.

But instead of it being the worst experience of her life, it hadn't been bad at all. As a matter of fact, she felt terrific!

"Daddy, I'm starving! Can we buy some popcorn now?"

Mr. Dapple laughed. "Sure! A box for the road can't hurt! I'm hungry, too."

Mrs. Dapple gave Margaret a hug, and the three of them stepped over to the counter.

☆ 10 ☆

As soon as Margaret got home, she rushed into Barbara's room and told her the whole story of meeting Naomi and Stephen at the movies.

"Can you believe they were there with her *mother?*" Margaret repeated for the third time. "I'm positive Stephen hates Naomi. Do you think he'll like me now?"

"I'm not so sure. You were there with *both* your parents!"

Margaret hadn't thought of that.

"So what should I do?"

Barbara crossed her legs and settled back on her bed. "This is your typical love triangle," she said. "It's in all the movies."

"Love triangle? What does that mean? Talk in language I can understand!"

"I'm sorry, but I gave up baby talk thirteen years ago." Barbara paused, waiting for Margaret's usual outraged reaction to one of her snappy remarks. But there was none. Margaret was too preoccupied to even realize she'd been insulted. "Anyway," Barbara continued, "here's how I see it. You, Naomi and Stephen are a love triangle. Do I have to draw you a picture?" Barbara picked up a pen and drew the following diagram:

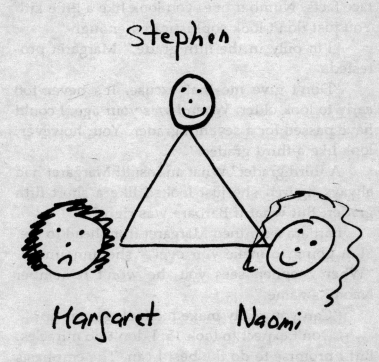

"Stephen is on top of the triangle. He's happy because two girls are crazy about him. Naomi's in one corner. She's smiling because she has something to be happy about. Stephen likes her. You're the sad one. He's not interested in you."

Margaret's eyes started to water. This was a pretty accurate assessment of her situation.

"I am the sad one." Margaret reached for a tissue on Barbara's bureau. "What am I going to do?"

Barbara looked very serious. "You have to face facts. Number one, you look like a little kid. You just don't look sophisticated enough."

"I'm only in the fifth grade," Margaret protested.

"Don't give me that excuse. It's never too early to look older. When I was your age, I could have passed for a seventh grader. You, however, look like a third grader."

A third grader? What an insult! Margaret had always figured she just looked like a short fifth grader. But what if Barbara was right?

Barbara examined Margaret from head to toe. "I'm going to make you over," she announced. "When Stephen sees you, he won't remember Naomi's name."

"Can you really make me look grown-up?"

"Don't expect to look 15. I don't do miracles. But I promise to do the best I can. The emphasis in beauty today, Margaret, is to make the most of what you have. And since you're a Dapple, you've got to have something!" Barbara smiled reassuringly.

Margaret looked at the array of make-up on

Barbara's bureau. She hated to admit it, but there were some things Barbara knew more about than she did. Maybe there was hope after all.

"We'll concentrate on bringing out your best features and minimizing your worst." Barbara cupped her hands into a frame like her father did when he was drawing and held them in front of Margaret's face. "You do have some good features. You have long lashes and your eyes are a nice blue." Margaret began blinking. "We'll emphasize them." Barbara drew her hands apart so Margaret's whole head could fit into her imaginary frame. "But your hair is disasterland. I'll have to do something with it." She looked Margaret straight in the face. "This won't be easy, but frankly, Margaret, without a real makeover you don't stand much of a chance with Stephen."

Barbara's words stung. But, of course, Margaret knew she was right. She'd been spending too much time on jacks and jump rope and not enough time on her appearance. She didn't even use a toothpaste with whiteners. How did she expect to attract a boy like Stephen?

"Will it work? Will Stephen like me?"

Barbara leaped up. "With the right make-up, a new hairstyle . . . I've seen it happen a hundred times." She began pacing back and forth. "A guy looks at a girl every day for years.

Nothing. Then suddenly one day he sees her as if for the first time. Why hadn't he noticed her before? Why hadn't he seen how beautiful she was? He must have been blind. What a fool he was!"

Margaret's heart was racing. Yes, that's how it would be with her and Stephen. What a fool he was!

"Margaret, when I'm finished you won't be the same kid anymore. There's going to be a new you!"

Margaret's heart was pounding. She wouldn't be a kid anymore! Those were the most wonderful words she had ever heard.

☆ 11 ☆

It was raining the following Sunday. It was coming down so hard that even with boots on your feet could get wet.

"This is perfect weather for our plans," Barbara exclaimed. "We have a great excuse for staying home all day."

Mr. and Mrs. Dapple were going to visit Margaret's grandparents who lived just a few blocks away. Then they were going out to dinner. They wouldn't be back until at least eight o'clock.

"Don't forget to finish whatever homework you have left before we get back." Mrs. Dapple pulled her umbrella out of the closet. "There'll be no TV for anyone who has homework to do!" This was a meaningful threat for Margaret. She loved Sunday night TV because it helped her forget she had to go to school the next day.

"Be good and don't mess up the house."

Margaret and Barbara exchanged looks. Would she ever stop?

Not just yet.

"Call us at Grandma's if you need anything," Mrs. Dapple continued. "Do you have the number?"

"Mom! We have everything. Go and have a good time!" Barbara opened the door for her parents. "Let me get the elevator for you."

"This is exceptional service," Mr. Dapple said, smiling.

"You're an exceptional father," Barbara replied.

"My girls are so terrific," Mr. Dapple beamed.

Mrs. Dapple buttoned up her raincoat and stared at Margaret and Barbara. "For now, anyway," she said.

The door was barely locked behind their parents when Barbara pulled Margaret into the bathroom. "Let's go. We haven't a second to waste."

Barbara examined Margaret under the bathroom light. She turned her head from side to side and pushed her hair back from her face.

"We'll begin with your mousy brown hair. It's boring and dull. I'm going to give it blonde highlights. It'll make all the difference."

"Blonde highlights?" Margaret was getting scared. "Isn't that too much?"

"Margaret, the way I'm going to do this, you'll just look like you spent a week at the beach. I'm going to create a subtle golden glow. People will know something is different about you, but they won't be sure what."

"Even Mommy?"

"She'll probably figure it out, but she'll have to admit it's a big improvement."

Margaret felt a little better. "I hope you're right."

"Remember, blondes are popular. They have more fun. I know what I'm talking about." Barbara began to comb Margaret's hair away from her face.

Margaret was thinking of all the times she had gone with her mother to her hair cutting salon. Her mother went to a place where they made you take off your clothes in front of other ladies and put on a robe. Margaret thought this was real creepy, but her mother didn't seem to mind. She drank lots of coffee there and read fashion magazines. They never had good kid magazines, but sometimes Margaret looked through *Seventeen*.

Margaret thought *Seventeen* was a strange magazine. Barbara read it and she was only fourteen. Tamara said her cousin Elissa read *Seventeen* and she was eighteen. Margaret once asked her mother how she would know when the time would be right to read it. Her mother had told her not to worry about it and to concentrate on reading books instead. Always the teacher. There

☆ 69 ☆

were also lots of ladies in the salon walking around with gook on their heads. They smelled really bad. Lots of them were becoming blondes.

"Sit down here," Barbara said, pointing to the toilet seat. Barbara went to the medicine chest and took out a brown plastic bottle. It was the stuff her mother used to clean cuts.

"What are you doing with that?" Margaret asked, checking her knees for scrapes. For once she didn't have any.

"This is going to give you subtle blonde tones. It's hydrogen peroxide."

How that stingy peroxide was going to make her a blonde was a mystery to Margaret. What if it burned her head? Barbara would have to blow on her like crazy! Margaret was getting nervous again. Her mother would be furious if she knew what they were doing.

"I don't know, Barbara . . . maybe this isn't such a good idea."

"Do you want Stephen or not?"

Margaret nodded yes.

"Then trust me and let me do my work. You are going to look so pretty Stephen will die!"

Barbara tore off a wad of cotton and soaked it with hydrogen peroxide. Then she began applying it to sections of Margaret's hair.

"We have to use just the right amount for just the right amount of time. Otherwise it won't come out right."

"How will we know?" Margaret began running her hands all over her hair. "Have you ever done this before?"

"Not to myself. But don't worry. A group of us used it on Toby Matthews, and she came out great!"

Margaret hated Toby Matthews. She had a big mouth, big feet and probably the biggest bra ever made. She always called Margaret "kid," and even Mrs. Dapple said she had a fresh mouth. So why would Margaret want to look like her? Except for the big bra.

The phone rang as Barbara was applying the last bit of peroxide to Margaret's hair. "Don't move! I'll be right back," she said.

As soon as Barbara left the bathroom, Margaret jumped off the toilet seat to look at herself in the mirror. Her hair was wet with hydrogen peroxide, and it still looked mousy brown. Margaret could hear Barbara gabbing on the telephone. She'd be on for a long time. Margaret began playing with the make-up Barbara had assembled on the sink. Some of it was Barbara's own Avon stuff for teenagers, but some of it was her mother's fancy make-up for grownups. Margaret went for her mother's stuff first.

First she put purple eye shadow all over her right eyelid. Then she added a dark green pearly eye shadow above it up to her eyebrow. Next she picked up a mascara wand and began applying black mascara to her lashes. This was trickier. Margaret's hand slipped, and the mascara smudged all over her eye. She'd have to do better with her left eye. For this one she chose a dark blue and a light blue shadow that came together in a small white compact. Deciding to skip mascara, Margaret added a little black eyeliner instead.

That did look dramatic. Lipstick was next. Out of the clutter of lipsticks Margaret picked one that came in a clunky bright gold case. She could see little pieces of herself in it if she held it real close. The lipstick was a bright orange called "Cagey Coral." She was carefully filling in her lower lip when Barbara walked into the bathroom.

"What have you done? You look awful!"

Barbara flung open the medicine cabinet and reached for her mother's cleansing lotion.

"We have to take all this off and start over again. Margaret, Margaret, Margaret," Barbara muttered as she rubbed tissues soaked in lotion over Margaret's eyes. "You're supposed to look grown-up—not like you're trick-or-treating."

"I was only fooling around. I knew it didn't look good."

Margaret's hands went to her head. "Hey! My hair feels like straw!"

"Your hair!" Barbara pushed Margaret's head

into the sink and turned on the faucet. She was mumbling something about mother and murder.

Margaret's heart was pounding. Was she going to be bald?

After briskly towel drying Margaret's hair, Barbara stood back.

"How does it look? How does it look?" Margaret was hopping up and down.

"Oh-oh . . ." Barbara covered her mouth. Her eyes were riveted to Margaret's hair.

"What's wrong? What's wrong?"

"Nothing. Nothing—it's just a little lighter than I'd imagined."

Margaret flew to the mirror. Staring back at her was a girl who most certainly did not have mousy brown hair.

"My hair's all blonde!" Margaret cried. "I can't leave this bathroom . . . ever!"

"Don't be silly. It's just the front mostly." Barbara turned Margaret's head from side to side. "I admit it's not exactly what I expected. But it looks good—really."

Margaret could not get used to her reflection. "Are you sure?"

"I'm telling you—it looks fine." Barbara fluffed up Margaret's hair and stood back again. "It was a little bit of a shock at first, but the more I look at it, the more I like it. You know, Margaret, I think you were born to be blonde."

Margaret looked deeply into the mirror. "Don't you think it's too blonde? Mommy will kill me."

"Don't worry. If she kills you, we're going together." Barbara parted Margaret's hair on the left and swept bangs across her forehead. "Let's not forget our goal here. Psychologically speaking, we're trying to jolt Stephen out of his complacent perceptions of you."

"What does that mean?" Margaret stopped fingering her new bangs.

"Meaning—shock treatment. That's what we're doing here. We're forcing Stephen to see you in a new way. So he can feel about you in a new way. It's basic psychology," Barbara said, tucking some hair behind Margaret's right ear and fastening it with a bobby pin. "There. That looks good." Barbara admired her work. "Sometimes the things you don't plan on turn out the best. This may have been your lucky day."

Margaret certainly hoped so. She returned to the mirror to see what Barbara had done. Looking at herself intently, she had to admit that her new hairstyle was quite becoming.

"See those blonde streaks in the front? Don't they look great?" Barbara was standing behind her.

Margaret lowered her head so that the light over the sink shone directly on it. Her hair did look sort of nice. It certainly looked glamorous.

"I guarantee one thing," Barbara said. "Stephen will notice you now."

What more could she ask for? Margaret reasoned.

Barbara motioned toward the edge of the bathtub. "Now sit here, and let me do your make-up. I'll use blusher to give you cheek bones. Suck in your face." Barbara applied two bands of brown rouge across Margaret's cheeks. "Your eyes will be next. And when I'm done, I don't want you to touch your face. Be in bed with the lights out when Mommy and Daddy come home. I'll make up some excuse for you. Tomorrow you'll get up early before anyone is up. And don't wash your face! Understand?"

"But Barbara, Mommy won't let me wear make-up to school!"

"You are such a nerd! Didn't you ever hear of sneaking out early?" Barbara shook her head. "I don't know how you made it to age ten. I really don't. And try to wear something decent tomorrow. It's your big day."

Barbara put her hands on Margaret's shoulders and stared deeply into her face. "Margaret, when you leave this house on Monday morning, I want you to remember one thing. You're going out there a kid, but you're coming back a star! Do you understand?"

"You really think Stephen will like me instead of Naomi?"

"I can only pity Naomi. She's lost him."

Margaret gazed at herself in the mirror.

"Sorry, Naomi," she said, smiling at her glamorous reflection. And with a toss of her head, she turned herself over to her sister's magic hands.

☆ 12 ☆

As Margaret entered the schoolyard, her heart was racing. Last night she felt like the most beautiful sophisticated ten-year-old girl in the world. But this morning, she could see there were black circles of make-up under her eyes, and her hair had so many of those "subtle blonde lights" Barbara had promised her that she hardly recognized herself. But she did look different. And she probably did look older. And maybe she even looked prettier. Maybe.

Margaret walked toward a group of girls playing jump rope. Would anyone notice how different she looked?

"Margaret, what happened to your hair?" Sandi Klein stood in front of her, a jump rope dangling from her hand. Annie Donat, the permanent rope turner because she was afraid to jump in, soon joined Sandi.

"Did somebody hit you? You look like you have black eyes."

Soon a group of fifth grade girls gathered around Margaret. Most of them were just staring at her. The rest were giggling. They were laughing at her blonde hair, her smudgy eyes, and her dark cheeks. Margaret was beginning to feel sick. This was not what she had expected. Not at all. Margaret walked into class and slinked into her seat. She pulled out a copy of *Scholastic* and buried her face in it. But it didn't help. She could still hear people giggling, and she could still feel all those eyes staring at her. Stephen was over by the bulletin board near the coat closet. So far he hadn't even looked at her. He and Julie Marshall were helping Mrs. Kopelman hang up the good compositions about U.N. Day. One of them was Margaret's. Maybe he'd never even notice how silly she looked.

"What happened to your hair? It's all orangey," Stephen said as he walked by Margaret's desk on his way to get more staples.

"Doesn't she look like a pumpkin?" Julie was laughing so hard her braces covered her whole face and those uneven braids were bopping up and down. Stephen laughed too. This was more than Margaret could bear. She ran out of the room and headed for the girls' bathroom. She locked herself in one of the stalls and sat down on the toilet seat. Then she cried. She could feel her make-up running down her face and her eyes stinging from black mascara. But still she cried and cried. How could everything have gone so wrong? She'd made such a fool of herself. Margaret blew her nose with toilet paper. She wouldn't stay in school a moment longer. She couldn't. She poked her head out of the stall door. No one was there. Mrs. Kopelman had probably gone for the Assistant Principal by now. Margaret sneaked out into the corridor. She ran to the rarely used exit by the art teacher's room. Safe. Flinging the door open, she raced down four flights of stairs. At the bottom of the last flight was the big heavy school door. Margaret leaned all her weight against it and pushed it open. She was out on the street. She couldn't hear the laughing anymore.

Now what could she do? She hadn't fooled anyone. To make matters worse, a truant officer or a policeman might pick her up and take her to the principal. She had to get home. If she ran, she'd only draw attention to herself. Margaret tried to walk casually—not too slow, not too fast. Her head was down so no one would see her face and laugh. As she walked by Kornblau's Hardware Store, Margaret had a terrible thought. How could she go home? She didn't have a key! Hadn't she been begging her parents all year to let her have her own key? But no—they said not until she was twelve. She was sick of being treated like a baby. But she didn't know how to be grown-up.

Margaret could see by the big clock over the Harlem Savings Bank that it was 9:30. She was already one-half hour a hookey player. She stood at the corner of Broadway and 181st Street and watched the light go from red to green three times. Grandma and Grandpa's! That's where she'd go. They'd be home! Now she was running. And she didn't care who noticed. Margaret ran into her grandparents' building and pushed the buzzer.

"Who is it?" a familiar voice came over the intercom.

"It's me, Grandma! It's me—Margaret."

Her grandmother buzzed her in. Without waiting for the elevator, Margaret rushed up the three flights to her grandparents' apartment. Her grandmother was standing by the open door.

"Margaret—what's wrong? Are you sick?"

Margaret held onto the banister to catch her breath. Her sneakers were untied and her hair had blown into her face. Margaret's grandmother took a good look at her.

"What happened to your hair?" Was that the only thing anyone could say today? "Who did that to your face?" That was the other. Her grandmother led Margaret into the apartment and sat her down at the kitchen table. She poured Margaret a glass of milk and sat across from her shaking her head from side to side. Margaret gazed around her grandmother's kitchen. She spotted the familiar shiny toaster oven, the blender with its Country Kitchen cover, and the yellow stepladder tucked in between the refrigerator and the sink. The sight of all these things she knew so well relaxed her. But Margaret's grandmother was not so relaxed.

"Now tell me what happened." Her grandmother stared at her. "Does your mother know you're here? Does your teacher know you're here? Margaret, Margaret," she muttered. Margaret pushed her milk glass away and told her grandmother all about how Barbara said she'd make her look pretty but how it didn't work and how everyone laughed at her. But she didn't tell her grandmother about Stephen. Some things were still a secret.

It wasn't too hard to convince her grandmother to let her stay home with her the rest of the day. By eleven o'clock a clean scrubbed Margaret Dapple was sitting in front of the TV watching reruns of "My Three Sons." She'd worry about everything later.

☆ 13 ☆

Later came at 3:30 that afternoon. Margaret was playing gin rummy with her grandfather. She was waiting for her winning jack of diamonds when her mother walked through the door. She looked mad. Margaret knew she was in big trouble. But before her mother could give it to her, her grandmother gave it to her mother.

"Phyllis, is this the way you take care of your children? I'm surprised at you!"

"Mom, Margaret left before we got up. I had no idea." Mrs. Dapple shot Margaret an angry look.

"You don't know how your children go to school? Don't you make breakfast?"

"Of course, I do. But I just told you Margaret sneaked out before breakfast."

"It's your job to be up before she is."

"Frankly, Mother, I don't need lectures on the care of my children." Margaret recognized her mother's angry voice.

"If you didn't, Phyllis, this would never have happened."

"Look, I really couldn't help what happened. And I don't want to discuss it anymore." Mrs. Dapple looked around the room for Margaret's coat.

"Ignoring responsibilities does not make them go away," her grandmother said. "I thought you were a better mother than this."

Margaret's mother said no more. But she had the same look on her face that Barbara had when Mrs. Dapple yelled at her for losing her keys.

Margaret didn't get a chance to tell her side until after she and her mother left Grandma's. They walked into the German bakery around the corner from their house. So far, her mother had been kind of quiet, but after buying some bread and black and whites, she seemed more ready to talk. "Suppose you tell me what happened." Her mother handed her the bag with the rye bread. Nibbling at a little end piece of bread, Margaret poured out her defense. She told her mother about Naomi and Stephen and how she had only wanted to be grown-up.

"Looking grown-up is not the same as being grown-up," Mrs. Dapple said as they walked toward the supermarket. "Growing up doesn't happen all at once. It happens a little bit at a time."

"I only wanted Stephen to like me. Anyway,

I'm sick of being a baby. I'm never allowed to do anything. I want to be able to do what I want whenever I want to."

"Do you think Daddy and I can do what we want whenever we want to?"

"Yes." Margaret was emphatic. "No one tells you when to go to bed or when you can go out or anything! You can do whatever you like!"

"That's simply not true." Margaret and her mother entered the supermarket. Her mother pulled out a shopping cart and headed for the dairy section. "No one can do whatever they like all the time. Growing up means responsibilities. And right now you have responsibilities too." Her mother put three yogurts and a container of milk in the shopping cart. "You have the responsibility to go to school every day—and *all* day, " she added meaningfully. "You have time to play and time to do work. There's time to be with us, time to be with your friends, and time just for yourself. But you're a part of this family, and you have to live by the rules of this family."

"Nobody else has as many rules as me!" Margaret protested as she tried to balance herself on the shopping cart. Seeing that it was about to tip, she jumped off, and she and her mother headed over to the check-out counter.

"Everybody has rules to follow. Even grownups. That's just the way it is."

"Well, I still can't wait to be grown-up."

Margaret let her fingers ride along with the food on the moving counter.

"It'll happen sooner than you think—or want!" Mrs. Dapple pulled out her wallet.

There was no winning with her mother. Even when she was wrong about everything, she always had the last word.

"Can I have some gum?" Margaret eyed the candy display in front of the counter. Surely she should get something for her suffering!

But "No!" was all she got. No gum, no candy, no! no! no!—that's all being a kid was about. No matter what her mother said, there was one thing Margaret was sure of. Growing up couldn't happen soon enough for her.

When Margaret and her mother got home, Barbara was sitting in the living room eating a gigantic red apple and reading the same huge book she'd been reading for weeks. It was called *Jane Eyre.* Barbara said it was about an exceptionally good and kind orphan who gets mistreated by everyone. It was her story, she said.

"Barbara, I'd like to talk with you—now." Mrs. Dapple put her groceries on the dining room table, hung up her coat, and sat down on the couch facing Barbara. Margaret sat on the floor by her mother's feet. "I think we have some serious things to discuss." Mrs. Dapple was leaning forward, her hands resting on her knees. "Things like dyeing your sister's hair and sending her to school with make-up. And things like making plans you know your parents won't approve of. Barbara, I'm so disappointed in you. How could you let your sister go to school looking like a clown?"

"She wanted to look more grown-up. I was only trying to help." Barbara defended herself.

"Look at her hair. Do you call that helping?" In the light of the living room, Margaret's hair had an eerie orangey-green cast.

"That was an accident. We can cover it up. I'll dye it back for her."

"No, thanks. You've done enough damage already. I'm sorry, but you're going to have to be punished."

"Why don't you punish Margaret? I did it for her. It's not fair! I get blamed for everything!"

"Your father and I will take care of Margaret." Margaret could almost hear the television being shut off. "But Margaret's still a little girl. You're the older one, and there are responsibilities that come with the privileges of being grown-up. I'm taking away your allowance for a week."

"My allowance! Then I can't go anywhere!" Barbara began to cry.

"Next time maybe you'll think more carefully about the consequences of your actions." Mrs. Dapple got up. "I'm disappointed in both of you."

"This is all your fault!" Barbara hissed at Margaret as she stormed out of the room. "I'll never forgive you!"

Everything was a mess. Everyone was mad at her. Why didn't things turn out the way they were supposed to? Margaret lay down on the floor. She was getting a bad headache. She rested her head on her arm and drew her knees to her chest. She'd had enough growing up for one day.

"Dawn, hurry up and finish writing today's register. I want to talk to the class."

Dawn Ellison, the class secretary, was standing on tippy-toe trying to reach the upper edges of the blackboard. She was writing down the names of the boys and girls who were absent as well as the class enrollment. Margaret was present today. And through a miracle called "shampoo-in hair color" she had mousy brown hair again. No one even seemed to remember Margaret the blonde. Maybe this was because the kids in her class were too nice to make fun of her. Or maybe Mrs. Kopelman said that anyone who made fun of Margaret Dapple would have to stay after school. Anyway, no one did, and Margaret was just as ready to forget the whole incident.

"I don't know why they let that tiny thing be class secretary," Margaret whispered to Tamara as she watched Dawn stretching up as far as she could. The top of the board was lost to her. Margaret was only about an inch or two taller than Dawn, but since she'd always been the smallest one in the class, meeting up with Dawn Ellison had been a dream come true.

"That girl has the neatest handwriting," Tamara marveled to Margaret.

"She drives me crazy. I hate how she writes. It's so perfect."

Margaret began mimicking Dawn's penmanship on the outside cover of her loose leaf.

Dawn the Yawn

she wrote in the tiniest, neatest letters she could. Tamara began to giggle. Dawn put down the chalk and returned to her seat.

"Thank you, Dawn."

Mrs. Kopelman's voice cut off all further jokes. Margaret put her hand over her version of Dawn's handwriting and looked straight ahead. Mrs. Kopelman got up from behind her desk, perched herself on the edge of it, and faced the class.

"As you know, it's time to hold new elections for class officers, and I think we should take care of this now. I'd like to open the floor for nominations for president, vice president, treasurer, and secretary. I'm sure you all understand how important these positions are. The people you elect will have many responsibilities and how they handle these responsibilities affects you. Let me remind you to please not nominate anyone who has already held one of these positions."

Margaret's heart was pounding. She had never held one of those positions. In the fourth grade she had been appointed stairwell monitor. That meant she got to yell at kids as they were coming up the stairs. She could even pull them off the line and make them wait until all the classes had gone up. But stairwell monitor was not an elected position. Class officer was something else. Maybe someone would nominate her! But what if she were nominated and then didn't get enough votes to win? That would be so embarrassing. Margaret pondered her dilemma.

Jeffrey Lippman, the old class president, was now in front of the room accepting nominations. Dawn was writing the names of the nominees on the board.

"Margaret, nominate me for president. Please!" Tamara was squeezing Margaret's arm. "I'd make a great president. If you nominate me, I promise I'll never tell on you if you're talking while Mrs. Kopelman is out of the room!"

"Tamara, that's not honest!" Margaret protested. On the other hand, it was an attractive offer. Jeffrey Lippman must have turned her in for talking at least twice a week.

"Okay, if you want, I *will* tell on you! Just nominate me!" Tamara was getting desperate.

"Only if you'll nominate me." The words were out before Margaret knew she had said them.

"It's a deal!" Tamara's hand shot up.

"Nomination for president from Tamara," Jeffrey called out.

"I want to nominate Margaret Dapple."

"Okay, nomination accepted."

Dawn neatly wrote Margaret's name under Kenny Kahn's and Susie Mishkin's. She was getting pretty close to the bottom of the board, since she could never use the top half. Good thing there were only four nominations in a category, Margaret observed through her panic.

"Raise your hand, Margaret, and nominate me!" Tamara was nudging her. "They'll only take one more name!"

Margaret's hand jerked up, but Jeffrey didn't call on her. He called on his friend Matthew Berger who nominated his friend, Max Elliot.

"All right. Nominations for president closed. Next category is vice president."

Margaret leaned over to Tamara. "I'm really sorry. I wanted to nominate you. I'll nominate you for vice president, okay?"

"Vice president? Are you kidding? I don't want to be vice president. My father says its the worst job in the country. I'd much rather be treasurer. Nominate me for that."

Treasurer? How could Tamara be treasurer?

She wasn't very good at math. How could she collect money for trips and the book club? She'd make a mess of everything! Margaret looked up and saw her name on the board for class president. Tamara's name should have been up there too. Maybe if she had raised her hand quicker, Jeffrey would have called on her. But it was too late now. She couldn't disappoint Tamara again. Maybe Tamara wouldn't be such a bad treasurer after all. Maybe they could do the math together.

Nominations for vice president were closed, and Jeffrey was moving on to the office of secretary. Margaret was no longer paying any attention. She was trying to figure out how many votes she might get. Max had a lot of friends, and Susie Mishkin was pretty popular. But Tamara would vote for her, and a bunch of the other girls might too. Maybe she could win. Margaret gazed at the world map over the blackboard. In her mind she was already class president. She was calling the class row by row—rewarding the good and punishing the bad. She'd be fair, not like some other creeps who had been president. Now she was walking down the aisle at assembly to accept awards for the class, all eyes on her filled with admiration. Stephen gazing at her as she strode by, sorry he never liked her. Being class president would be great!

"Nominations for treasurer now being taken."

Margaret raised her hand immediately.

"Margaret, nomination please."

"I nominate Tamara for treasurer."

"Nomination accepted."

Dawn wrote down Tamara's name. Jeffrey quickly accepted three other nominations for treasurer and declared all nominations closed.

"Thank you, Jeffrey and Dawn." Mrs. Kopelman was back in front of the class. "We'll elect the president first. Will the candidates please leave the room."

Margaret got up. Her knees were shaking. She was scared to death. I'll never win, she told herself. Only Tamara will vote for me. Why didn't I refuse the nomination? Tamara smiled at Margaret as she filed out of the room with Kenny, Susie, and Max.

The four nominees gathered out in the hallway. Margaret was trembling. Susie was staring hard at Class 5-2's bulletin board on haikus. Max was pacing up and down. Margaret looked at Kenny. He looked even more scared than she did.

"I know I'm not going to win," Kenny whispered to Margaret. "Only Adam will vote for me."

"Don't worry," Margaret said. "I'm not going to win either. Only Tamara is going to vote for me."

"No way, Margaret!" Kenny replied emphatically. "Lots of people will vote for you. You'll win."

"Are you crazy, Kenny?" Margaret was

amazed. How could Kenny think she was so popular? Still she was flattered. Somebody thought she was popular. Suddenly Margaret wished she could vote for Kenny.

Kenny was standing with his hands in his pockets. His shoulders were hunched forward, and he was staring hard at his shoes.

"If I don't win," Kenny began without looking up, "I'm not going home."

"Why?" Margaret asked, wondering how the vote was going inside.

"My father will hate me." Kenny was still not looking at her.

"Why should your father hate you?"

"He says I never do anything right. He was class president three times when he was a kid. And now he's vice president of his company!"

Big deal! Margaret thought to herself, having recently learned that being vice president was a big nothing. Susie had stopped her tenth reading of the same poems and was now listening to Margaret's conversation with Kenny.

"Fathers always say things like that," Susie offered. "I bet he was lying about being class president."

"He was not!" Kenny said angrily. "I'm not going home if I lose. I'll only get punished."

Get punished for losing an election? Margaret couldn't believe it. Some kids had it worse than she did! Her parents certainly wouldn't punish her if she lost. Barbara would probably say that the kids in the class had good taste, but that was about the worst she could expect. Everyone would still love her. She was sure of that. Poor Kenny.

"I wish the election were over." Kenny was pale and sweaty. "I can't stand this."

At that moment Stephen opened the door. "Come on in. We're finished."

Margaret's heart sank. The four candidates filed back into the room—Susie, Max, Margaret, and Kenny, dragging his feet.

"Hey, Kenny," Margaret heard Stephen whisper as they walked past him. "You only got one vote!"

Kenny's eyes filled with tears. They began to stream down his face. Margaret just gaped at Stephen. How could he have said that? Margaret couldn't bear to look at Kenny. How could Stephen have been so mean?

Margaret's concern for Kenny had made her forget her own interest in who won, but as soon as she entered the room her eyes hit the blackboard. Susie's name was circled as the winner. She was jumping up and down. Margaret murmured her congratulations and took her seat.

"Margaret," Tamara squealed. "You almost won—Susie only got two more votes. And you know Daisy and Julie had to vote for her because they go to her summer house every year."

Margaret barely heard Tamara. She was in a state of shock. Two votes! That's all.

"Let's face it," Tamara continued philosophically. "My mother always says most elections are bought."

"Who voted for me?" Margaret was determined to find out just who her friends were. She'd be extra nice to each of them.

"I'll tell you later. We have to concentrate on the election for treasurer!"

Margaret went through the motions of voting for people for vice president and secretary, but all she could think about was how close she had come to being president. From time to time she would check on Kenny. He was staring hard at his ruler trying not to look as if he had been crying. Poor Kenny. Margaret felt so bad for him. And Stephen didn't even look sorry. Margaret faced the front of the room again and tried concentrating on the rest of the election.

"Treasurer's next." Tamara leaned over to Margaret. "Don't forget. Vote for me!" Tamara got up to leave the room.

"Hey, Tamara," Margaret called after her. "Practice your timestables out there!"

"If I win, I'm making you my assistant!"

Lucky Tamara to have me as her assistant, Margaret thought as she raised her hand to vote. After all, I almost became president!

☆ 15 ☆

As if almost being class president weren't good enough, Margaret found a party invitation waiting for her when she got home from school. She could tell it was an invitation before she even opened the envelope. It was just the right size for either an invitation or a thank you note. And since nobody owed Margaret thanks for anything, it had to be an invitation. She ripped open the envelope. Sure enough, inside was a card with a frog holding a balloon that read "You're Invited." Margaret, pleased with her powers of deduction, opened the card to see who the invitation was from.

In the space next to where it said, "Given By" was the answer. Written in a combination of script and print was the name, "Naomi Finer." So Naomi was having a birthday party. Margaret re-read the invitation. It was going to be held next Saturday at 5:00 P.M. Margaret knew she was free. She went into her room and propped the invitation up against the lamp on her night table. It was nice to be invited to a party—even if it was Naomi's. Since that afternoon at the movies, Margaret didn't feel so angry with her. And a party would be fun—soda, candy, dancing with her friends. Margaret could hardly wait. She ran to the telephone to call Tamara to find out if she knew who else had been invited.

On the third ring, Tamara's mother answered the phone. Before letting her speak to Tamara, she asked Margaret the usual questions parents ask.

"How are you, Margaret?"

"Fine."

"How's school?"

"Good."

"How are your parents?"

"Fine, thank you."

"Tell them I said hello."

"Okay."

Finally she put Tamara on the phone.

"Hi, Margaret. I was just thinking about you."

"Oh, yeah? What were you thinking?"

"I was thinking that maybe you could explain to me how to figure out the sales tax on the books from the book club. Now that I'm treasurer, I have to understand everything."

Tamara was certainly taking her job seriously. Margaret was impressed.

"That's easy. You make the percent a decimal, multiply it with the cost and add the amount to the price. Got that?" Tamara was silent for a few seconds.

"I think I'll use a calculator." Tamara quickly changed the subject. "Did you get your invitation to Naomi's party?"

"Yes, I did. Who's coming?"

"She invited the whole class! Isn't that great?"

"The whole class? Where's everyone going to sit?" Margaret was picturing the Finer's small living room.

"You worry about everything! We can always sit on the boys' laps!"

The boys' laps?

"What are you talking about, Tamara? Boys are coming to this party?" Margaret was stunned.

"Of course. That's what's so wonderful!"

So wonderful? Margaret was speechless. How could Naomi have a party with boys? That was ridiculous. What would they do at a party with boys? What games would they play? Hadn't Naomi learned she was too young to fool around with boys?

"Tamara, this party is going to stink."

"What do you mean? It's going to be great. Do you think Adam will kiss me?"

Adam kiss Tamara at the party? This was getting worse by the minute. Even though Margaret had already noticed that she didn't feel so weak when she saw Stephen (and after his meanness today, the thought of him made her more mad than wobbly), she still did not want to be at a party with him. Or any other boy, for that matter. She'd have a horrible time at this party. Maybe if she was real lucky, she'd break a leg by next week.

Margaret spent the rest of that week hoping something disastrous would happen. But as Tuesday turned to Wednesday and Wednesday turned to Thursday, Margaret's hopes turned to dread. Her leg was holding up nicely, and even her A— on her book report didn't help her feel better. Of course, she was quick to observe that from now on she'd have to get Barbara to help her every time. But what was an A in social studies next to an F in social life? What was she going to do? A party with boys. What was the matter with her friends? Girls always had such a good time together. Why did they want to mess it up with boys?

Tamara had called Margaret about six times to discuss what she was going to wear. Boys always liked Tamara. Margaret attributed this to her extensive wardrobe and her more grown-up appearance. After all, Tamara could almost wear a little bra. But Margaret had nothing. Even Barbara called her "pancakes." What if the boys called her that?

On Thursday night Margaret stood in front of her mirror eyeing herself. She placed her hands on her hips and threw her head back, trying to look sexy. She lowered her eyelids ever so slightly and pouted. That's how all those ladies on the covers of fashion magazines looked. Somehow Margaret knew she didn't look the same. Margaret tossed her head, turned to the left, and jutted out her chest. Nothing! She looked ridiculous. Margaret placed her fingers over the front of her top and gathered the material into two points which she stretched out. She stood back to see the results. So this is what she'd look like with a bust! Not bad! Suddenly Margaret had a brainstorm. She ran to her drawer and pulled out two pairs of knee socks. She rolled them up into little balls and stuffed them under her shirt. She rushed over to the mirror to admire her transformation. She had breasts! Once again, she put her hands on her hips and threw back her head. Very sexy! Now she looked like the ladies on the covers of those magazines her mother was always hiding.

"Margaret! What are you doing?" Barbara was standing in the doorway, her eyes glued to Margaret's bulging socks.

"Margaret! You're a scream! From pancakes to apples! Mommy's got to see this!" Barbara threw herself on Margaret's bed, tears of laughter streaming down her face. "My sides are going to split!"

Margaret was beet red. "Shut up! You witch!" She lunged over at Barbara, her arms raised over her head. Oh God! Her socks were falling out! Barbara was shrieking with laughter. One pair of socks was already on the floor and the second pair was nestled in the middle of Margaret's waist.

"Margaret! You have a breast growing on your stomach. Better see a doctor!"

"Get out of here, Barbara!" Margaret was purple. "Get out of here!"

"I'm going, sexpot! I'm leaving!"

Margaret was standing by her bed crying. "Just get out of here!"

"Don't worry. I'm going." Barbara was in the doorway, her hand on the doorknob. "Just one piece of advice. Next time try tissues!"

Barbara raced out and quickly slammed the door behind her. And just in time. Because two pairs of socks were flying toward her head.

☆ 16 ☆

It took Margaret a few days to get over her humiliating episode with Barbara. If being flat-chested weren't bad enough, a sister who tormented you about it certainly was. Mrs. Dapple had tried her best to convince Margaret that, 1. being flat-chested was not a permanent condition; 2. some women *never* get big breasts and are perfectly happy; 3. Margaret would not be a baby her whole life; 4. boys would like her for who she was and not for how sexy she looked; 5. it shouldn't even matter so much if boys liked her or not anyway, what she was as a person was the most important thing; and 6. Barbara was not adopted, and she couldn't be returned even if she were.

Margaret could not really accept any of her mother's statements as true with the exception of number 6 which she admitted to herself with great reluctance. She was stuck with Barbara and a flat chest.

If only Naomi weren't having a party everything would be okay. Why did she have to have one anyway? She probably just wanted to brag about being eleven! Margaret wouldn't be eleven for another six months. No wonder Naomi kissed boys. Being eleven probably made you boy crazy. Naomi was in the wrong grade. Maybe she'd been left back in kindergarten because she was too dumb to play with blocks. What a blockhead! Margaret chuckled at her little joke, but when she stopped laughing she could see her own situation hadn't improved much.

After much debating about what to wear to Naomi's party, Margaret settled on her blue plaid blouse and her brown corduroy pants. She knew she hardly looked like a Junior Sophisticate. This was the name of the line of clothes Tamara's father manufactured. He promised Tamara that when she got bigger she could have all those clothes, and Tamara was just waiting for that great day. Margaret did have a nice denim jumper that her mother had let her pick out a few weeks ago, but she didn't feel like wearing it. Why bother dressing up for this crummy party?

Barbara was prancing around the house in her bra and underpants, getting ready for a party she was going to. Her date was picking her up, and Mr. and Mrs. Dapple were straightening up the living room so that Barbara's date wouldn't think her parents were slobs. Barbara was now in the bathroom doing her usual number in front of the mirror.

"My face is so broken out!" she wailed. "I can't go anywhere!"

Barbara was obsessed with pimples. Mrs. Dapple said all adolescents got them, and Margaret always figured that was one good reason for not growing up. Barbara was carefully examining a pimple in the middle of her chin. She had a specially prepared lotion from the skin doctor that was supposed to make pimples disappear. It came in a white glass bottle with a yellow top, and though the doctor had convinced Barbara that it was better than any make-up she could buy, it certainly didn't seem to be helping much. As far as Margaret could tell, that pimple was still there.

"It's time for surgery," Barbara muttered, grabbing two tissues and wrapping her fingers in them.

"Don't touch your face!" Mrs. Dapple poked her head into the bathroom. She was doing her usual trick—the appearance from nowhere. "Leave your skin alone or you'll get scars!"

Barbara scowled.

"Don't worry, honey. No one will notice it."

"Are you kidding?" Barbara groaned. "It's almost the size of my whole face!"

"No, it's not," Margaret cut in. "It's almost

the size of your whole brain!" Margaret snickered. That would get her back for "pancakes."

"That's very funny, Margaret. Do you do funerals?" Barbara patted more pimple medicine on her face. "So is Stephen coming to this party?" Barbara spoke to Margaret's reflection in the mirror of the medicine cabinet.

"I guess so. But I don't care."

Barbara turned to face her. "That's a switch. What happened?"

"Stephen made a boy in my class cry, and he wasn't even sorry."

"So he's mean, huh?" Barbara rubbed a little rouge on her cheeks. "He's probably covering up a deep-seated neurosis. It's better to know these things early, Margaret. Why waste your time with a sicko. Right?"

"Yeah." This time, Margaret thought she even knew what Barbara was talking about. "Right!"

When Margaret was all set to go, Mrs. Dapple handed her a gift for Naomi. Margaret hadn't even remembered. Gifts were usually the first thing she thought about when she had a party, but why should she bring Naomi a present? Naomi was making her miserable and she had to bring her a gift?

"How would you like it if Naomi came to your party without a gift?" her mother persisted.

Margaret knew she'd be pretty insulted if

that happened, but she didn't want to tell her mother that. Instead she grumbled, "I hope you didn't buy her anything too good."

"I bought her a game, and I hope she likes it."

Margaret reluctantly took possession of the gift-wrapped rectangular box her mother held out to her.

"Margaret, I know Naomi likes you very much. And her mother is such a delightful person."

Why should her mother think Naomi was nice just because her mother was?

"Now go and have a good time. Tell me all about the party when you get home. And don't worry about the boys. They're just as afraid of you as you are of them."

Where did her mother get her information? Boys afraid of girls. That was a laugh!

By the time Margaret dawdled over to Naomi's house, the party was already under way.
Some records were playing, and Tamara was
dancing with Annie. Everyone else was hanging
around the living room drinking soda and eating
pretzels and potato chips. The girls were on one
side of the room, and the boys were on the other.
Spotting her friend Adrienne over on the couch,
Margaret went to sit next to her. Adrienne was
real nice. She never said mean things to people,
and she once lent Margaret her lucky pen for a
math test. Margaret knew she would have failed
without that pen. Adrienne was also very tall,
but Margaret liked her anyway. Adrienne didn't
look too thrilled with this party either. By now,
a lot of the girls were dancing together, and the
boys were still standing around. Naomi was
dancing with Bonnie Sue Walden, her best friend
from summer camp. Bonnie Sue was a whole year
older. She had long, wavy black hair and big blue

eyes with long lashes. She wore perfume. If there was anyone who made even Naomi look like a baby, it was Bonnie Sue.

Margaret was beginning to relax. So this was what a party with boys was like. Same as with girls, only more crowded! Margaret was munching on some corn chips and telling Adrienne how she was thinking of organizing a fifth-grade jacks tournament. When her favorite record came on, Margaret started dancing with Adrienne. The boys weren't bothering her at all. Mrs. Finer was talking to them. She's probably asking them to leave, Margaret thought smugly. Then Mrs. Finer began gesturing toward the girls. Suddenly Margaret knew what Mrs. Finer was up to. She was telling those creeps to dance with the girls. Stay out of this, Mrs. Finer! Go talk to your husband!

It was too late. Stephen walked over to Naomi and started dancing with her. It spread like the bad cold everyone in Margaret's family had last winter. Soon Adam was dancing with Tamara, Billy was dancing with Susie, Peter was dancing with Daisy, Dave was dancing with Sharon . . . Margaret couldn't stand it anymore. What if a boy came over to her? What if a boy didn't? Margaret and Adrienne took one look at each other and stopped dancing. Adrienne ran to the bathroom. Margaret sat down on the couch and tried to look busy. She picked up the candy dish next to her and stared hard at the chocolate-covered raisins in it. The candy dish was made out of mosaic tiles. Margaret figured Naomi must have made it in camp. Some of the tiles had been glued in crooked, but it wasn't a bad job. Margaret concentrated on each raisin as if there were something mysterious about it. If she didn't look at anyone, maybe no one would come up to her.

"Margaret, do you want to dance?"

Margaret looked up, a chocolate-covered raisin melting over her index finger. Matthew Berger was standing in front of her.

"Do you want to dance?" Matthew repeated.

Margaret was so stunned by Matthew's invitation that her mind went blank. She heard herself say, "Okay," and she followed him numbly to the middle of the room. Matthew began dancing immediately, but Margaret's feet were barely moving. What was she doing dancing with Matthew Berger? Where did he pop up from? Did he like her? Oh God, Margaret hoped not. Margaret looked at all her friends dancing. Did she look ridiculous to them? She must. She felt so ridiculous. She didn't know where to put her eyes. It was too embarrassing to look at Matthew. Did he think she was a good dancer? She felt so awkward. With her eyes averted downward, Margaret could see Matthew moving around on the dance floor. He was swinging his arms in front of him and shaking from side to side. He was avoiding looking at Margaret. That was nice of him. She could pretend she was dancing with Adrienne. She decided to just ignore him too and get through the record. As soon as it stopped, Margaret began to move toward the couch. But another record came on right away, and Matthew just continued dancing. She couldn't leave him dancing alone. She was stuck again! Matthew started talking about the rock group they were dancing to. He said his father worked for a big record company and he had gotten Matthew all the group's record albums. For free. That was a pretty good deal, Margaret commented. As they fell into silence again she noted to herself how her parents' jobs never got her anything good. A teacher and an art director. Speeches on neatness, and don't touch Daddy's art supplies. You'd think her father could have gotten her free crayons or something. Margaret was beginning to feel more relaxed. Matthew was a good dancer—for a boy. At least he didn't do anything embarrassing like jump around too much or look stupid. When the music stopped, Margaret stood there waiting for the next record to drop. She really was having a good time. Now that she was calm enough to think, it occurred to her that Matthew was kind of okay. He was a little taller than she was. He had dirty blonde hair and big green eyes. He was actually very cute. And very nice too. Why hadn't she paid attention to him before? He had been class president last year, and he was one of the best the class had ever had. He was fair. He put anyone who deserved it on the bad list—even his friends. Now that was unusual! Margaret was beginning to feel very good about Matthew Berger. She was even beginning to hope that he liked her.

The new record began. Oh-oh. This record was slow. Margaret knew all about slow dancing. She'd seen teenagers dance slow on TV, and once when Barbara had a party at the house she peeked in the living room and saw everyone dancing. Boys had their arms around the girls, and their bodies were touching. It was disgusting. Some people even kissed. Yuck!

Margaret did not want to put her arms around Matthew. Or any boy for that matter. She took a quick glance at Matthew to see what he was going to do. He seemed very flustered. Oh, please, Margaret pleaded silently. Don't ask me to dance again.

"Do you want some soda, Margaret?" Matthew had stopped dancing. They stood facing each other, the only still couple on a floor of people moving closely together. "I'm very thirsty."

Matthew wasn't going to ask her to dance slow!

"Yes, I'm very thirsty too." Margaret was overjoyed.

Matthew led the way into the kitchen. It was big and quiet and empty. Maybe this was worse. Now she'd have to talk to him—alone. There were six big soda bottles lined up on the kitchen table with flowered paper cups stacked between them. Margaret looked for the black raspberry, but since it hadn't been opened yet, she poured herself a cup of ginger ale. Her hand was shaking. Soda spilled on the table and trickled down to the floor. There was no way to clean it up without Matthew noticing. Margaret tried covering the spill by stepping on it.

"Do you see any ice?" Matthew was holding a cup of soda in his hand.

"No. I don't see any."

"I hate warm Coke." Matthew put his cup down. "Do you think Mrs. Finer would mind if I looked in the freezer?"

"I'm not sure." Margaret's mother had told her it was rude to help yourself in someone else's home.

Margaret could see a little puddle of soda seeping out from under her big toe. Maybe Matthew would think she made in her pants! This was awful! Why didn't someone else come into the kitchen? Wasn't anybody else thirsty? Please God—send someone in here—now! God must have liked Margaret because just then someone did enter the kitchen. But God couldn't have been too crazy about Margaret because it was

Bonnie Sue. Margaret instinctively stepped to the side. She remembered a story Tamara had told her about Bonnie Sue wanting to be a model and how she had sent pictures of herself in designer jeans to all the big modeling agencies. Bonnie Sue said she knew she'd be rich and famous one day. She even practiced signing her autograph: "My love to you, from Bonnie Sue." Margaret was more scared of Bonnie Sue than she was of Matthew.

"I'm starving. What's there to eat around here?" Bonnie Sue began flinging open kitchen cabinets.

Suddenly Mrs. Finer appeared in the kitchen, a newspaper tucked under her arm. "Can I get you something, Bonnie?"

"I'm hungry. Do you have something to eat?"

"How about a nice apple? Or a banana?" Mrs. Finer examined the contents of her refrigerator.

"No, thank you. I only eat crud. Do you have any bar-b-que potato chips? I just love those. Don't you?" Bonnie Sue turned a big smile on Matthew.

"I'm sorry, Bonnie." Mrs. Finer wiped up the spilled soda by Margaret's foot. Margaret could feel her cheeks burning. "I don't have any bar-b-que chips. There are regular ones in the living room. Why don't you eat those?" Mrs. Finer removed two apples and some swiss cheese from the refrigerator, arranged them on a wooden plate and carried her snack out of the room.

"Is she kidding?" Bonnie Sue turned to Matthew. "Those chips don't even have ridges!" Bonnie Sue tossed her thick black hair behind her shoulders. "That woman is real cheap!" She filled a cup with soda and headed back to the living room.

"Do you want to go back too?" Matthew asked Margaret.

Since there wasn't much point in hanging around the kitchen, Margaret followed Matthew back to the living room. As soon as they neared it, she noticed something was different. There was hardly any light coming from the room, and there were no records playing. Peering into the darkness, Margaret saw everybody sitting in a circle on the floor.

"What are you doing?" Margaret asked in a little voice.

"We're playing spin-the-bottle," Billy whispered excitedly. "Come on in."

Margaret was stunned. Spin-the-bottle was a kissing game.

"Naomi's mother thinks we're telling ghost stories!" Tamara giggled.

"It was my idea," Bonnie Sue volunteered. She was perched on her heels, her hands resting on her thighs. She looked gorgeous. And grown-up. "Matthew, come sit by me." Bonnie Sue made a space for Matthew between her and Adam.

She wants Matthew! Just when she had gotten to sort of like him. Margaret noticed Adrienne and Julie sitting on the couch. They weren't playing. Julie probably didn't want anyone to kiss her braces. Margaret couldn't blame her. Adrienne was fooling around with an insta-matic camera. She aimed at people and took their picture.

"Wait till it gets really good," Bonnie Sue called out to her. "Then you can take my picture!"

Margaret stood on the edge of the circle. She could just join Adrienne and Julie on the couch. She wanted to so badly. But everyone probably thought she was such a baby already. She couldn't embarrass herself anymore. She took a breath and sat down next to Matthew. Maybe she'd get to kiss Stephen. Margaret felt sick. Or maybe Matthew. Margaret turned to look at him again. He really was cute. Cuter than Stephen.

Bonnie Sue was explaining the rules. "If you're a boy and you spin to another boy, you can shake hands or forget it. Same thing for girls to girls.

"For the first round, hold the kiss for one count, for the second round, two counts, and so on. You can kiss on the cheek if you want (Good, that's what I'll do, Margaret consoled herself) but that's for kids. (Margaret felt ill again.) Lips is much better."

How would she survive? Plus, even if she did, her mother would kill her later. Margaret knew her mother would never approve of her playing kissing games. She was always telling her kids were growing up too fast. That was the stupidest thing Margaret had ever heard, but still, if she found out . . .

The bottle was spinning. Billy to Dave. They decided to just forget it. Then Billy spun again. Annie Donat. Now how was a girl who was afraid to even jump rope going to let a boy kiss her? Margaret's eyes followed Billy as he walked over to Annie. He bent over, and by the count of one, he had kissed her on the lips. Everybody giggled. The bottle kept spinning. So far only girls had spun at Margaret. Then it was her turn. She twirled the bottle and as it spun, she chanted silently, "Point to a girl. Point to a girl."

The bottle stopped. Matthew. It was pointing straight at Matthew Berger. The fourth round. Four counts with Matthew. A fantasy flashed through Margaret's mind. Her father was at the door. Let's go, Margaret. It's time to go home. But she was still in Naomi Finer's living room and an empty Coke bottle was pointing at Matthew. Matthew turned to her. He placed his hands on her shoulders. Margaret closed her

eyes. She couldn't bear to look. She felt his lips on hers. 1 . . . . 2 . . . . 3 . . . . 4. Then it was over. Somebody was spinning the bottle again. Margaret wanted to touch her lips, but she was afraid if people noticed they would laugh. Matthew had kissed her. A boy had kissed her. She could still feel Matthew's kiss. And she thought she always would.

☆ 18 ☆

Although Margaret was very tired when she got home from Naomi's party, she was also elated. She kissed her mother hello and went to her room to get into her pajamas.

"Is Barbara home yet?" Margaret called.

Her mother appeared in the doorway. "No. She's still at Lisa's party. I'm sure she'll be home soon."

How could Barbara stay out so late? Margaret wondered. She was exhausted!

"Too bad. I wanted to tell her about the party."

"Did you have a good time?" Mrs. Dapple began hanging up Margaret's clothes.

"Yes, I really did."

"That's nice," said Mrs. Dapple, picking up two comic books off the floor. "What did you do?"

"We drank soda, listened to records, danced, played a kissing game . . ."

"A kissing game?" Mrs. Dapple stopped cleaning up.

"And somebody kissed me! Somebody really nice. He kissed me on the lips!" Margaret was bouncing on her bed.

"I'm glad you had a good time, but you know, I think you're a little too young for kissing games."

Margaret frowned. Was her mother going to spoil everything?

"I only kissed once."

"Well, that should hold you for a few years!"

"It's not something you want to do every day anyway," Margaret said.

"No, I guess not." Mrs. Dapple tucked Margaret in.

"Would you tell Barbara to wake me when she comes home?" Margaret said.

"I think it'll be too late. You can talk to her tomorrow."

"Okay," Margaret turned over on her side. "Don't forget to tell her I want to talk to her."

"I won't." Mrs. Dapple bent over to kiss Margaret. "Good night, honey. See you in the morning."

"Good night, Mom."

Mrs. Dapple turned off Margaret's night light and gently shut the door. Margaret listened to her mother's footsteps growing fainter down the hallway, and then she heard her call, "Alan, I have to talk to you!"

Margaret lay in bed with her eyes wide open. She couldn't stop thinking about the party. It had been so exciting. She pictured herself dancing with Matthew. Did he like her? Did he like kissing her?

Margaret got out of bed, turned on her light and went over to the window. There was her school building just a few blocks away. It was too bad P. S. 187 always ruined her view. She quickly looked at the apartment buildings across the street. The lights shining through some of the windows made the faces of the buildings look like a giant checkerboard. What was happening in all those bright apartments? What were all the grownups doing? No one was telling them to go to bed. Were they watching the late show? Or were they having company and eating party food on little breads?

Margaret's eyes rested on a row of darkened windows. Was everybody in those apartments asleep? Or were they at parties? Or sitting in fancy restaurants with flowers on the table? The noise of a car pulling up in front of her building drew Margaret's attention. She watched a couple get out of a taxicab. She could hear their laughter as they hurried into the building. Would she ever be able to go out on a Saturday night and stay up as late as she wanted?

Margaret moved away from the window and sat cross-legged on the edge of her bed. She imagined herself grown-up and on a date with Matthew. They were coming home from a movie, and it was so late that even her parents and Barbara were fast asleep.

The sudden noise of the washing machine stopped Margaret's fantasy. Her parents' voices came floating above the rumble of the machine. Then Margaret made out a third voice. It was Barbara's. Margaret jumped up and opened her door a crack. It was hard to figure out exactly what Barbara was saying since she was talking with her mouth full. But there were giggles coming from the kitchen. Barbara must have had a good time. She heard Barbara say good night to her parents and then she saw her coming down the hall.

"Barbara!" Margaret poked her head through the door.

"What are you doing up?" Barbara turned towards Margaret's room.

"SSSH! You want to come in and talk?" Margaret whispered.

"Shouldn't you be asleep?" Barbara looked over her shoulder toward the kitchen.

"I'm not tired. Come in—please!"

Margaret quickly shut the door behind Barbara who sat on the floor and leaned against the bookcase.

"So what's up?" Barbara swallowed a yawn. "How was the party?"

"I kissed a boy!"

"You're kidding!" Barbara sat straight up. "Was it Stephen?"

"Stephen! Uggh!" Margaret shuddered. "It was someone much better. Matthew Berger."

"Who's he?"

"He's our old class president. His father gets free records. He's very nice."

"Did you tell Mommy? Is she going to let you go out with him?"

"I don't know. Do I have to?" The thought of actually dating Matthew made Margaret nervous.

"I guess maybe you're too young." Barbara stretched out on the floor.

Margaret was relieved. Kissing Matthew had been exciting. But dating. . . . She could count on her mother to veto that.

"So Naomi wasn't so dumb inviting boys after all."

Margaret thought about this for a moment.

"She's okay, I guess," Margaret said. "But inviting boys was just lucky."

"Lucky for you!" Barbara twirled the ends of her hair. "And you almost didn't go to that party! I told you—sometimes the things you worry about most turn out okay."

That was really true, Margaret thought. She

lay back on her pillow and crossed her arms above her head. She'd worried about seeing Naomi and Stephen at the movies, and that turned out okay. She'd worried about running for class president, and she almost won. She'd worried about looking too young, and now it didn't seem to matter. No one even remembered her blonde hair. She'd worried about Naomi's party, and she had a great time. Margaret sat up.

"Want to play Monopoly?"

"Monopoly? Are you for real?" Barbara pulled herself off the floor. "That takes forever." Barbara kissed Margaret good night. "I'm going to bed. See you tomorrow."

Barbara crept out of Margaret's room, softly shutting the door. But Margaret was still restless. She got off her bed and returned to the window. The streets were quiet. There were hardly any lights on anywhere. Was everybody sleeping? Margaret yawned widely. She got back into bed and reached over to turn off her light. Then she stopped. No, she would leave it on. And if someone somewhere got up in the middle of the night, they would see her light. And maybe they would stand by their window and wonder what she was doing.

Margaret snuggled under the covers. Her eyes kept trying to shut, but she wouldn't let them. She imagined herself grown-up. She was standing behind a desk giving very hard tests.

Margaret smiled. Yes, maybe she would be a teacher. Or maybe a movie star. And maybe married. Maybe to Matthew. Margaret's eyes were just too heavy to keep open. In a few seconds she was fast asleep. And up and down Ft. Washington Avenue, from the park to Fred's candy store, hers was the last light shining.

ABOUT THE AUTHOR

LINDA HIRSCH, a native New Yorker, lives with her husband in northern Manhattan. She has an M.A. in English literature from the State University of New York at Stony Brook, and she teaches at Hostos Community College of the City University of New York. Her first book for children, *The Sick Story*, was, as *Publishers Weekly* put it, a "wryly humorous" tale which "any youngster could appreciate," and became a Weekly Reader Children's Book Club selection.

Ms. Hirsch says *You're Going Out There a Kid, But You're Coming Back a Star* was inspired by her own childhood experiences. "But Margaret is braver than I was," she admits. "I spent my first spin-the-bottle game hiding in the bathroom."

Now you can have your favorite **Choose Your Own Adventure**® Series in a variety of sizes. Along with the popular pocket size, Bantam has introduced the **Choose Your Own Adventure**® series in a Skylark edition and also in Hardcover.

Now not only do you get to decide on how you want your adventures to end, you also get to decide on what size you'd like to collect them in.

SKYLARK EDITIONS

☐	15309	The Green Slime #6 S. Saunders	$1.95
☐	15195	Help! You're Shrinking #7 E. Packard	$1.95
☐	15201	Indian Trail #8 R. A. Montgomery	$1.95
☐	15190	Dream Trips #9 E. Packard	$1.95
☐	15191	The Genie In the Bottle #10 J. Razzi	$1.95
☐	15222	The Big Foot Mystery #11 L. Sonberg	$1.95
☐	15223	The Creature From Millers Pond #12 S. Saunders	$1.95
☐	15226	Jungle Safari #13 E. Packard	$1.95
☐	15227	The Search For Champ #14 S. Gilligan	$1.95
☐	15241	Three Wishes #15 S. Gilligan	$1.95
☐	15242	Dragons! #16 J. Razzi	$1.95
☐	15261	Wild Horse Country #17 L. Sonberg	$1.95
☐	15262	Summer Camp #18 J. Gitenstein	$1.95
☐	15270	The Tower of London #19 S. Saunders	$1.95
☐	15271	Trouble In Space #20 J. Woodcock	$1.95
☐	15283	Mona Is Missing #21 S. Gilligan	$1.95
☐	15303	The Evil Wizard #22 A. Packard	$1.95
☐	15305	The Flying Carpet #25	$1.95
☐	15318	The Magic Path #26	$1.95
☐	15331	Ice Cave #27	$1.95

Prices and availability subject to change without notice.

Buy them at your local bookstore or use this handy coupon for ordering: